AMERICAN

DREAM

ISBN:0979040094
ISBN-13:9780979040092

This book is dedicated to all
the therapy and service animals
in this country and to the people
who selflessly train them to enrich
the lives of others. And to Zia,
who has provided so much comfort,
joy and laughter, we wonder how
we ever got along without her. And to
my family - Scott, Andy, Jordan and
Rob, thank you for all the support and
encouragement.

ACKNOWLEDGMENTS

I wish to thank K-9 Comfort Dog Ministries for the chance to visit with their beautiful Golden Retrievers in Illinois. The dogs are therapy animals that have been service trained. The dogs and their handlers have traveled to places such as the Boston bombings and Sandy Hook, Connecticut, providing comfort to victims and families and bringing a smile to a child's face in the aftermath of horror.

I also wish to thank the countless other non-profit organizations that provide service and or therapy animals to those in need. Several of these groups have mentioned that 'it's like magic,' when they bring an animal together with a person in need, which is where I got the idea for the name Magic in the story.

Webb

Webb

Chapter 1

Anna saw the new neighbor for the first time as she rushed out the door with her son Nathan in tow. If she was late for work again this week, she was afraid Mr. Jones would fire her.

"Hi, I'm Brian Chase," the handsome neighbor said as he crossed the street and extended his hand. She took in the moving truck backed into the drive of the mobile home directly across from hers. She took his hand, looking him over as she did. Wavy brown hair curling just over his collar, broad shoulders stretching the black tee shirt tight across his chest.

"I'm Anna James." She felt a warm tingle as he took her hand gently in his. Her eyes locked with his and she was mesmerized for a moment. His eyes were a steel blue. Somewhere between blue and grey, she thought.

"This is my son Nathan," she said when she could finally tear her gaze away.

"Hi Nathan, it's nice to meet you," Brian was surprised as the boy only stared at him, unmoving.

"I don't mean to be rude," said Anna, "but I'm late for work and I still have to drop Nathan at Mrs. Wilson's across the street. Welcome to the neighborhood," she called over her shoulder.

Anna thought of the stranger again as she drove her old Ford pickup to the grocery store where she worked. *Man, he is gorgeous, and the way he stared at me. So intense. And his wavy brown hair and sexy blue eyes must drive the girls wild.* She smiled. "Brian," she said out loud as she pulled her truck into the grocery store parking lot. Anna had been alone a lot this past year. She used to be so alive and vibrant.

Now she felt like a hollow shell of her former self. She felt empty inside and only drifting through life, survival was her only plan for the future.

Not that she hadn't had offers. She had been asked out numerous times when the cowboys from the ranches came through her line at work. They were all so polite and gentlemanly, tipping their cowboy hats to her, but she couldn't think about dating. Not for a while, at least. In fact, if she were to admit it to herself, she was afraid to get involved with anyone after what she had been through. She couldn't imagine building a life with someone again, only to have it ripped away from her in an instant. She was still trying to adjust to a completely new life and raising a small, troubled son on her own. They both seemed to be adrift in a deep blue sea of their own sadness and mourning. She wasn't even sure where the past year had gone. She had only made it through one day at a time, never thinking of the future or making any plans.

As she pulled her trusty old pickup into

her drive after work, Anna could see Nathan playing on the swing in Mrs. Wilson's yard.

She walked across the street and over to son. Nathan looked up as she neared, but didn't smile or speak.

"Hi sweetie, ready to go home?"

The boy nodded as he crawled out of the swing. She took his hand and went to let Mrs. Wilson know she was back. Mrs. Wilson was an elderly widow who had been caring for her son since she moved to the trailer park a year ago.

"He's already eaten dinner," Mrs. Wilson assured Anna as they went out the door.

"Thank you, Mrs. Wilson," she replied. "Let me know what you need from the store tomorrow and I'll bring it on my way home."

"Oh, Anna." Mrs. Wilson caught her before she made it out the gate.

"Remember my grandson I told you about?"

"The one in Afghanistan?"

"Yes. He's supposed to come home on

leave soon and I would like for you to meet him. I think he would be perfect for you. He's just about your age."

"Thank you, Mrs. Wilson and I look forward to meeting him, but I'm really not looking for a date right now."

"See you tomorrow," she called back as she herded Nathan through the gate.

Nathan continued to play quietly in his own yard while Anna went to take a shower. He loved playing in the sandbox she had built for him.

She had just stepped from the shower and wrapped a towel around herself when she heard a knock at her door. Anna ran to the door in her towel, her long honey colored hair dripping down her back. She assumed it was Mrs. Wilson. Nathan must have left something at her house.

"Hi." A slow grin spread across Brian's face as he took in her slender form dripping on the rug. His gaze traveled from her long dripping hair to her bright hazel eyes, then continued down to her slender hips and long slim legs. Then, his eyes moved just as slowly back up her body to meet her confused look, his grin still in place.

"Seems like you need a new latch for your gate," he said. " Your son chased a stray dog out into Main street."

"That's impossible," Anna's voice sounded angrier than she had meant it to. She looked past the few trailers in the park to the town's main street beyond. She shuddered at the thought of her little boy running into that busy street. It was a main route between Amarillo and Denver, filled with big trucks and cattle haulers.

"I'm sorry, but he's never been able to open that gate," she said in a softer tone.

"Maybe you forgot to latch it?" Brian lifted an eyebrow.

"Puppy," Nathan said barely above a whisper.

"Honey, did you open the gate to chase the puppy?" Nathan looked at his feet and nodded. Anna realized she was still standing in the door in a towel, water running down her back from her long hair. She blushed and stammered, "thank you for bringing him back, Brian. Would you like to come in? Could I offer you a cup of coffee or a beer?"

"Coffee does sound good," he replied. "I'm still on duty, so I can't have alcohol." For the first time she noticed his dark uniform with CFD stenciled on his tee shirt. She also noticed how the navy blue shirt looked almost too small for his broad chest and shoulders. He wore black boots and black cargo pants with the bottom tucked into the boots. The overall effect of his outfit was incredibly sexy, she thought. She looked back up to find him smiling at her again.

"Carson Fire Department," he said as she blushed again. "I noticed you were trying to read my shirt."

Anna gave an embarrassed nod as she saw the amusement in his eyes and for the second time, she realized she was still in a towel.

"I'll just put something on and then we can talk." She turned and almost ran down the narrow hall to her room.

Brian shook his head, still grinning and went to check on Nathan. The child was sitting on an old brown couch in front of the television.

He appeared to be six or seven years old. Shaggy, blond hair, huge blue eyes. Cute kid, Brian thought as he sat on the couch beside him and asked, "whatcha watching?"

Nathan ignored him completely. *Ok. Let's try yes or no questions.*

"Do you like dogs?" He tried again. The boy's head swiveled around to look at him.

"Puppy," he muttered.

Just then, Anna came back into the room wearing jeans and a loose tee shirt, her long mane of honey colored hair still damp.

"How about that coffee?"

"Sure," Brian heaved himself off the worn sofa.

Jeez, he's tall, and that gorgeous wavy hair. Embarrassed at her thoughts, she knelt in front of the boy on the couch and hugged him to her. He looked away from the T.V., but didn't return her hug, Brian noticed.

"Don't ever go outside the yard without Mommy there, o.k. Nathan?" He nodded, eyes back on the T.V.

Brian followed Anna to the kitchen and sat at her small table while she put a pot of coffee on.

The kitchen of her small trailer was open to the living room. It's green and white patterned linoleum giving way to an ugly green shag carpeting in the living room. Dark paneling ran the length of the small trailer. Anna had hung bright colored prints and posters on every wall.

But the dark, dingy trailer is still pretty depressing, he thought.

She brought two cups of coffee to the table and smiled shyly at Brian as she took a seat. She didn't have many visitors, *especially not one who looks like a movie star,* she smiled as she looked him over again when she thought he wasn't looking.

"How long have you lived in Carson?" Brian asked as he added cream and sugar to his coffee.

"One year this month. We moved out from Denver. And you?"

"I grew up on a ranch near here, but I haven't been around much the last couple of years."

He looked at her quizzically. "Why would you leave the big city for this small cow town?"

Anna sighed. "I grew up in Denver and married my high school sweetheart. Nick was a contractor. He built houses and I sold real estate. We were living the American Dream...you know," she said at his puzzled look, "big house, nice cars. I spent more money decorating that house than this entire trailer is worth." She shook her head ruefully. "At the time, I thought it was what I wanted."

"And now... what do you want now?" Brian asked softly. He was staring at her with such intensity, it made her even more nervous.

"I just want my son back," she hung her head and waves of honey brown hair fell forward covering her face. Brian glanced over at Nathan. The trailer was so small, he was really only a few feet away. He was still engrossed in an old rerun T.V. show and paying no attention to them.

"Does he have autism?" Brian asked quietly.

"No. PTSD. Post Traumatic Stress Disorder," she said at Brian's puzzled look.

"He was fine until last year. A happy, normal little boy. Then, the housing market crashed and Nick's company went under. I lost my job a few months later." She paused, stirring her coffee absentmindedly. "I'm sorry, I don't usually talk about my past. I tell everyone my husband passed away and we needed a change of scenery."

"It's o.k. Anna, you can talk to me. After all, we are neighbors now, right? There can't be any secrets in a trailer park this small," he chuckled. "And, I knew you were a widow.

It's a small town. Everybody knows everybody, right? I've seen you a few times at the store, but never got a chance to speak to you."

"Well," Anna began uncertainly, "after we both lost our jobs it was really only a matter of time before we lost the house too. We both tried so hard to find any job we could." Tears welled up in her eyes as she relived her nightmare. "We were able to rent a camper in a trailer park and we bought a small car with the last of our savings. Nathan was four and a half. We couldn't pay for daycare anymore so we took turns staying with him and looking for work. We had been searching for eleven months when…" she paused when she saw the look on his face, "please don't feel sorry for us," she begged him. "I can't stand pity. It's a recession, other people have been through worse than our family."

"I won't," he smiled kindly at her. "Sounds like you're a tough lady. What about family? Parents, brothers, sisters?"

"My parents sold everything a few years

ago and moved to Florida. They're on a fixed income. There's no way I would burden them." She sighed heavily.

"And no, I don't have any brothers and sisters." Anna had been stirring the coffee in her cup as she talked, which had long since grown cold. She looked up, locking gazes with him again. The intensity of his piercing grey-blue eyes caused her to squirm in her seat. She couldn't tear her eyes away from his.

Finally, he lowered his eyes, refilling his cup from the coffeepot she had placed on the table between them.

"Go on," Brian urged.

"Nick was killed by a drunk driver," she continued, the pain and anger evident in her voice. "Nathan was with him." Almost a whisper now, Brian leaned forward to hear her. "It was a head on collision. Nathan was the only survivor. We don't know what he saw or heard in the time before the ambulance arrived. And he doesn't tell us. Since then, he's been quiet and withdrawn.

He was always a little shy, but now he hardly speaks at all. He saw a grief counselor for a while in Denver, but it made no difference."

Brian shook his head slowly as he thought about what she'd been through.

"A couple of months after the accident, I saw an ad online for a job opening in a grocery store. I was fortunate enough to get the job. We had just enough money from Nick's life insurance for the Ford truck and the move. And we've been here ever since. I don't know what's come over me," Anna said in disbelief. "I haven't told our story to anyone here. Not even Marcie."

"Is that the Marcie that works at the grocery store?" He was staring at her again with that strange intensity, his eyes locked onto hers.

"Yes. She's really the only friend I've made since I've been here."

"Until now," he put his hand over hers on the table, still staring into her eyes. She jumped slightly, and then relaxed. It had been so long since a man held her hand. His hand was big and warm and work roughened.

"Thank you, Brian." She meant it. She hadn't meant to unload on him, but it really had felt good to be able to talk to someone.

"Where did you move from?" Anna was more than happy to shift the conversation to him.

"I transferred from Springfield. I've had to wait over a year for an opening in the Carson fire department. My parents have a ranch south of town and I wanted to be closer to help them out when they need me."

"That's nice of you," Anna said. "Have you been a firefighter long?"

"Only a couple of years. My friend Jason helped me get into it. We grew up together and we always talked about being firemen. My dad wanted me to stay and help with the ranch; I figure this way, I can do both. He wants me to learn more of the business side of ranching."

"Mmm…Sounds nice," Anna was enjoying the conversation more, now that the focus was on him.

"Well," Brian caught her off guard when he stood up from the table. "Guess I better get back to work before the fire station sends out a missing person report. I'm on evening shift this week. Perhaps I could stop by again sometime?"

"Anytime," Anna smiled up at him, then she stood too and walked him out.

"See ya later, slugger," he called to Nathan, who hadn't moved from the couch. The boy didn't reply, but his eyes met Brian's for an instant before turning back to the T.V.

Brian drove back to the fire station, still thinking about the things she'd told him about herself and Nathan. He was used to being around wounded kids and maybe he could even help, but he was not so sure about Anna. She was still getting over the loss of a husband and the life she had known.

He didn't want to do anything to cause her any more pain than she had already been through. The pain and sadness he'd seen in her hazel eyes had made him want to sweep her up and carry her away from all her problems. Maybe I can just be a friend, he thought. A shoulder to lean on.

Yet, even as he thought it, he saw her waves of long, honey-colored hair and those long, lean legs. He had wanted to grab that towel and rip it from her body.

And the heat he felt run through his body every time their eyes locked. He grinned and shook his head to clear it as he pulled into the fire station.

The rest of the week went by with no sign of Brian. Anna tried to put the tall, sexy stranger out of her mind, but she kept seeing those intense eyes, staring right through her, his gorgeous sandy brown hair curling over his collar.

She found herself listening for a knock at the door every evening as she moved about the kitchen, making dinner for Nathan and herself.

And she caught herself glancing across the street at his empty trailer as she came and went.

You're not dating, remember? She scolded herself. *Forget about him.*

She had started dinner Friday evening when she heard a knock at her door. Her heart pounded and her hand trembled slightly as she reached for the knob.

But it was her friend and coworker Marcie, smiling at her as she opened the door. Anna felt her heart sink a little as she returned the smile, glancing across the street to Brian's house before stepping back to invite her friend in.

"I just stopped by to see if you want to get a sitter and go into Denver with me?"

"Marcie, you know I'm not into the downtown club-hopping scene."

"I know, but I have to keep trying. You never go anywhere or have any fun. You need to let your hair down a little."

"I'm sorry, but I'm really not interested. But you could stay for dinner with us."

"No thanks Anna, I'll grab something in

town."

She gave Anna a quick hug and left, never glancing at the quiet little boy in front of the T.V.

Chapter 2

The clerks at Ranchland Foods rotated weekends. This was Anna's weekend off and she was catching up on housework Saturday morning. Nathan was playing in his sandbox as usual.

She could see him from her window as she did the dishes in her small sink. He was pushing his little cars through the sand and crashing them together, over and over.

She finished at the sink and moved on to the living room, picking up Nathan's toys as she went. Anna's heart nearly stopped when she heard Nathan's high pitched squeal from the yard.

She raced out the door, leaped off the wooden trailer steps and slammed into Brian. He hit the ground on his back with her on top of him. She jumped frantically to her feet, still searching for Nathan.

She saw her son on the ground a few feet away, a large black puppy crawling over him and licking his face. Nathan squealed again in delight.

She looked back at Brian, he had made it to a sitting position. He was looking up at her and laughing.

"Why did you tackle me like a line-backer?" He asked, still laughing.

"I'm sorry, Brian," she laughed nervously as she dropped onto the grass beside him, blushing. "I ran out the door so fast, I didn't see you. Where did the puppy come from?"

"I don't know," he answered. "I was washing the fire trucks out in front of the station this morning and the little bugger just appeared at my feet. I didn't notice him running around the neighborhood while I was working. It was like magic, all of a sudden, there he was."

She could feel her pulse slowly returning to normal as he talked.

They watched Nathan rolling around on the grass with the puppy and laughing.

"Oh, my God," exclaimed Anna, "he's laughing!"

"Magic," Nathan said as he looked up at Anna and Brian and smiled happily.

They sat in the grass together for an hour watching Nathan run and play and laugh with the black puppy.

Finally, Brian stood and helped Anna to her feet. She noticed how his biceps bulged against the sleeves of his tee shirt as he pulled her up.

"I've gotta get back to work," he said.

"I've been helping out this week in northern Colorado with a wildfire, now I've gotta finish cleaning and putting away equipment."

"Brian," she grabbed his arm as he was turning toward the gate. "I can't thank you enough for the puppy.

It's been so long since I last saw Nathan laughing and having so much fun."

"Come have fun with me tomorrow," Brian said unexpectedly. "One of the guys from the station is having a barbeque. He has a big family, it should be a lot of fun."

She hesitated , "I don't know, Brian. We can't just invite ourselves along."

"You're not, I'm inviting you," he laughed as he went through the gate. "See you tomorrow then. One o' clock." He jumped into his jeep before she could protest any further. She smiled and waved as he drove away.

Nathan wouldn't go to bed that night without his puppy. Anna finally relented and let the puppy sleep on a rug beside his bed.

"I love you sweetie," she said as she hugged Nathan and tucked him into bed. He met her eyes and smiled.

"Magic," he said.

"Did you hear Brian earlier?" she asked.

"The puppy appeared as if by magic?" He nodded eagerly. "Magic," he said again.

"You want to call him Magic?"

"Yes," he said, "Magic."

The pup looked up from his spot on the rug

and yipped once.

"I guess he agrees," she laughed. "Magic it is." He really is a pretty black dog, she thought as she closed her son's door half-way. Maybe a Labrador or Lab mix. Let's just hope no one comes to claim him.

She thought about Brian again as she lay in her own bed. *I wonder why he invited us to a barbeque?* She hadn't done anything fun since they'd been in Carson. She and Nathan had fallen into a routine of quiet evenings and weekends at home, each lost in their own separate mourning. She had tried talking to Nathan about his dad, but it only seemed to make the boy more withdrawn. She smiled as she remembered Nathan rolling in the grass with the puppy. I haven't seen him laugh in a year. Thank you, Magic puppy. She drifted off to sleep with the smile still in place.

Brian couldn't sleep that night as he lay in bed in his hot, stuffy trailer. The air conditioner was broken and he hadn't got around to telling the landlord, Mr. Cranston, about it. He hadn't planned on asking Anna to the barbeque. It had come out of his mouth before he realized it.

He smiled in the dark as he thought about seeing the trailer door fly open and Anna landing on top of him. He would have been happy to stay right there on the ground with her on top of him if she hadn't been in such a panic over her son. I don't need to get mixed up in this, he kept repeating to himself. This lady has enough problems without me getting involved. Yet, he knew he wanted to spend more time with her. He wasn't sure what it was about her, other than the physical attraction. Of that, he had no doubt, but he knew there was something more, he felt drawn to her in a way he had never known before. Was it her shy, unassuming ways or the deep love he could see in her eyes when she looked at her son.

He thought there was happiness and laughter buried just beneath the surface, but she'd kept it hidden for so long, maybe she just needed help finding it again.

Sunday was a beautiful Colorado summer day. The huge cottonwoods formed a shady canopy over the small trailer park. The Arkansas River drifted lazily along just behind the mobile homes.

Anna sat in a lounge chair in her small yard reading while Nathan sat in the sandbox with Magic. He seemed to be having a one- sided conversation with the dog. Magic stared at him as if he was hanging on every word, wagging his tail occasionally.

Anna was trying to concentrate on her book, but her thoughts kept slipping back to Brian. *What an amazing guy.* The puppy had brought the first real signs of joy to her son's face that she had seen in a year. For that, she knew she would be forever grateful to Brian. He's not too bad to look at either, she smiled to herself. She thought about his wavy brown hair and piercing blue eyes. He must be over six feet tall, she thought.

Just then a shadow fell across the page she was supposed to be reading. She looked up to see Brian's tall form looming over her. She blushed, hoping he couldn't read her mind.

"You two ready for some fun?" he asked.

"Sure," Anna answered as she stood up from her seat on the lounge.

"You ready to go Nathan?" The little boy was still deep in conversation with his dog.

"Can I bring Magic?" he asked.

"Magic?" Brian looked confused. Anna laughed. "Yesterday, you said the puppy appeared at your feet..."

"Like magic!" Brian finished for her.

"Nice name, Nathan," he laughed too, his blue eyes dancing. "And yes, if it's o.k. with your mother, the Jeffries have a fenced yard. Magic will love it there."

It was a short drive to the Jeffries house. Nathan held Magic on his lap in the back seat of Brian's car, talking incessantly to him.

Anna felt happier than she had for a long time. She hadn't heard this many words from her son for an entire year.

Jason and his wife Brenda were warm and welcoming to Anna and Nathan. They both seemed to be about the same age as her. Twenty eight or nine, she guessed. Jason was shorter than Brian, thin with dark hair and a mustache.

Brenda was slim and attractive with shoulder length blonde hair.

They led the way to the backyard where three noisy children ran to them. Nathan stood shyly with Magic in his arms as the children ran to see the new puppy.

"This is Brendan, Michael and Skyler," Brenda introduced her children as they excitedly fired questions at Nathan.

"What's his name? How old is? Where'd you get him?" They all said at once.

"His name is Magic," Nathan said proudly as he set the pup down. "And that's how we got him, it was magic."

"Cool name," Brendan said.

The kids all ran to the swing set, Magic trailing at their heels as Brenda invited Anna to sit at a picnic table.

"Hey Anna," Brian dropped down beside her at the table. "I didn't want to say anything in front of Nathan, but a lady showed up yesterday afternoon at the fire station looking for a black puppy."

"Oh," Anna felt her heart sink as her eyes followed Magic chasing the swings back and forth.

"Hey, "he said gently, "It's o.k. I bought him."

"You what? How?"

Brian laughed. "The animal shelter is on the street behind the fire station. I guess she left a gate open and the pup took off. I went back with her and paid for him. I have all his paperwork in my Jeep for you. At least no one will come looking for him now."

"Brian, you have to let me pay you back. I'll make payments, whatever it takes."
Brian started shaking his head no, then stopped, a mischievous grin spreading slowly across his face.

"O.K., dinner once a week for a month. I don't get much home cooking, you know."

"It's a deal," she shook his hand and her eyes locked with his again, the strange intensity of his blue-grey stare making her uncomfortable.

Brenda turned away to hide her smile. She knew Brian could cook better than anyone she knew. She also saw the way Brian's eyes slid to Anna when he thought she wasn't looking. She had known him for a long time and she had never seen him look at a woman the way he looked at Anna.

Brian went to help Jason with the grill while Anna told Brenda about Nathan's depression. She didn't give too many details, but Brenda could see Nathan was watching her children more than playing with them. "It takes time," she told Anna. "The puppy will help."

"It already has. He's been talking more and laughing. Brian has been a godsend."

"And for you?"

"I don't know. I guess I've been in a bit of a fog the past year. One minute my life was all planned out and the next minute, it's all gone. I've just been getting by, not thinking about the future."

"Brian is a good guy and I can see he likes you. He'll understand if you're not ready yet."

"Thanks, Brenda. The physical attraction is definitely there, at least on my part."

"Yeah, you and half the town, right? You know girls love a gorgeous fireman?" They both giggled as Brian and Jason came back with their hands full of food.

"You ladies gonna help or just sit there giggling about us behind our backs?" Jason joked.

"We're going, we're going," Brenda

laughed as Anna blushed a deep red when she saw the knowing grin spreading across Brian's face.

After lunch, Brian wrestled in the grass with Brenda's kids. They piled on top of him and wrestled him to the ground, Magic jumping and barking at the excitement.

Anna was surprised when Nathan suddenly ran and joined in the fray, piling on top of the kids on top of Brian. He squealed in delight as Brian grabbed him an tickled his sides. *Was this her same sullen, shy child of the past year?*

Brian climbed from underneath the children, grabbing the youngest, Michael, as he went, swinging him in circles around the yard.

Everyone laughed as each child wanted a turn. Nathan ran to Brian, "me next, me next," he called. He squealed delightedly as Brian swung him around and around until he was dizzy. When Brian put him down, he ran to Anna.

"Did you see me swing, Mommy? Did you see me?"

"I saw you," she replied as she gave him a hug.

"I'm glad you're having fun, sweetie."

The afternoon went by much too fast. The children played with Magic until the puppy was exhausted. Anna hated to see the day end. It was wonderful to see her son run and play. He had been completely withdrawn around other children the past year. He usually hung back and watched from the sidelines as other children played. Even in school, his teachers had been worried about his unhappiness and depression.

Magic slept on Nathan's lap on the way home. Anna stared at Brian in awe as he drove. This wonderful man and magical puppy had brought a bit of happiness to their lives after a long, sad year of barely existing.

"Would you like to come in for coffee?" Anna asked Brian as he turned into her driveway. She didn't know about him, but she personally didn't want to see the day end.

"Sure," he said as he lifted a sleeping Nathan off the seat. Anna took the puppy from him and unlocked her door.

They put Nathan to bed together and Magic on his spot on the rug beside the bed.

"Fun day, mommy," Nathan said as she tucked him in. Brian smiled as he watched the two of them together.

Over coffee, Anna asked Brian, "What about you? I've told you everything about myself and I know hardly anything about you.

"That's not true. You know I love kids and dogs," Brian joked.

"Come on, you know what I mean. Tell me about yourself. Did you go to school here in Carson? Have you ever been married?"

Brian hesitated. "I was adopted," he finally said. "I grew up and worked the ranch with my adoptive parents, but I always wanted to be a firefighter. I want to help people the way my parents helped me. My parents take in foster children at the ranch." Anna's eyes grew wide in surprise.

"They have three right now. Two of those from troubled homes," he said.

"They give kids a second chance at life."

"Wow." Anna was amazed. "They must be wonderful people."

"They are. Why don't you come see for yourself. Are you and Nathan free next weekend?"

"Yes," Anna said. "I only work every third weekend. We would love to go."

"To answer your question, I grew up on the ranch, went to school right here in Carson and I guess I just never found the right woman. Before," he said as he took her hand. She looked into those intense blue eyes and knew she couldn't tear her gaze away this time. He pulled her to him as he leaned forward over the table. Brian let go of her hand and put his big hand on her face, sliding it slowly to the back of her neck. He kissed her lips so gently, so softly, she felt shivers run up and down her spine. Anna was left breathless and trembling slightly. *Is this man good at everything he does?* Never had she known a kiss so gentle, yet so intense.

"Nice," he said. He rose from his seat slowly, smiled and winked at her. Then he turned and went out her door.

"What the hell?" Anna said aloud.

She sat at the table for a while, thinking about Brian and the effect he was having on her. He was so easy to be with, yet his good looks and intense gazes still made her feel nervous. She had to admit to herself, when he had kissed her with such intensity, she had definitely wanted more. She had known her late husband since high school and after all the years they had spent together, she couldn't remember a time when she had felt her knees go weak from a kiss. Of course, she had loved Nick very much. It just seemed to her now that they had spent so much time working on their home and careers, maybe they hadn't taken the time to really enjoy each other.

Chapter 3

Nathan wouldn't go to Mrs. Wilson's without Magic and Anna didn't have the heart to say no. The puppy had brought such a change in the boy. Mrs. Wilson said she would love to have Magic too.

"I lost my old Cocker Spaniel before you moved here," she told Anna. "I've missed having a dog. I would've looked for another dog already if I didn't have Nathan to keep me company."

She tousled the boy's hair as he went to her swing, Magic at his heels.

When Anna arrived at the grocery store, her friend Marcie cornered her.

"I hear you're dating Carson's most

eligible bachelor?"

Anna thought she detected a note of jealousy in Marcie's voice.

"Who told you that?"

"It's a small town, Anna. There are no secrets."

"Well, it's not true. Brian has never asked me for a date."

"Oh," Marcie seemed somewhat placated.

"We just went to a barbeque at his coworker's house."

"And?"

"And nothing. It was a nice day. Nathan had a great time playing with Brenda's kids."

"Oh, well, I'm glad you're finally getting out of the house."

Anna nodded, confused. Marcie hadn't sounded glad at all.

She'd even sounded a little angry.

Marcie went back to her register leaving Anna with an uneasy feeling. She finally shrugged it off, thinking she must be imagining Marcie's jealousy. She knew

Marcie spent a lot of time in Denver, she was always talking about the *city guys* she had hooked up with. She doubted Marcie would be too interested in a small town guy.

Anna was running her register and bagging groceries when she felt someone staring at her. She looked up and Brian was in her line, a slow grin spreading across his face as she nodded at him.

"Hi Anna," he said as she started scanning his items. "Would it be o.k. if I stop by this evening?"

"Sure," she smiled and blushed, feeling like a schoolgirl under his steady gaze. She glanced over to see Marcie at her register glowering at her.

Uh oh, now I've done it, she thought dejectedly. She *is* jealous and I just made it worse. She took Brian's money and made change nervously, not sure if it was his nearness that unnerved her, or the weight of Marcie's stare.

Marcie seemed to avoid her the rest of the day, then she left before Anna had a chance to speak with her.

Brian came by after work and she invited him to stay for dinner.

"I owe you dinner, anyway," she told him.

He went out to the yard with Nathan while she cooked. She watched them out the window as she moved about the kitchen. Brian was showing Nathan how to train Magic. They were teaching him to sit. Magic seemed to be catching on fast. Anna had to admit, the black pup was quickly stealing her heart, too. He seemed to be just what Nathan had needed to heal. He talked to the dog more than he'd spoken to anyone in the past year.

After dinner, Brian and Anna sat over coffee in the kitchen while they watched Nathan working with Magic. Nathan held a dog toy in the air. Magic stood on his hind legs, begging. Nathan circled the toy in the air and Magic spun around on his hind legs.

"He's going to be very easy to train," said Brian. Anna nodded, her eyes still on her son.

"Nice job, Nathan," Anna laughed softly and they both clapped their hands as Nathan beamed. Then Nathan dropped to the floor, giggling as Magic bounced around him, trying to lick his ear. It was wonderful to watch her son with his dog and the change it was bringing out in him. After a year of near silence, she could see he was slowly coming out of his shell. Her heart filled with pride as she watched the boy with his dog.

Brian finished his coffee and left after giving Nathan and Magic a hug. Anna walked him to the door, but he didn't try to kiss her or make a move toward her. It left her feeling confused and uncertain. She had been sure that she didn't want any relationship, but now she found herself yearning for his kiss. His beautiful steel-blue eyes and wavy hair crept into her thoughts at night as she tossed and turned in her bed, trying to clear her mind enough to sleep. She was confused at her own emotions. After a year of numbness, the physical attraction she felt for Brian surprised her.

Brian began coming by every evening after work. He and Nathan were training Magic. Anna invited him to dinner but he didn't stay. Nor did he try to kiss her again. I guess we're just gonna be friends, she frowned as she thought about it. Nathan wouldn't let Brian leave every day without a hug and he had to give Magic a hug, too. Anna could see the little boy was becoming very attached to him. And so am I, she had to admit to herself.

But why did he never kiss me again? Should I take the initiative or does he only want friendship and I'll make a complete fool of myself? She was surprised at herself, but she was beginning to lose sleep at night. She tossed and turned, Brian's beautiful face creeping into her thoughts constantly.

Brian's thoughts were on much the same path as he left the two of them every evening and crossed the street to his lonely trailer. He was determined to take it slow with Anna and be a friend to her. But damn it, he didn't know how long he could hold himself back. Anna didn't even seem to realize how beautiful she was. He wanted so badly to tangle his hands into her long mane of hair and kiss her until she begged for more. He hadn't been able to get her off his mind since he met her. He had been looking for a sign from her that she wanted more than friendship, but so far, he hadn't seen it. Although that kiss had told him a lot. There was so much fire and passion in her kiss, he knew he'd had to get out of there quick or not at all. *Damn it!* He gave up trying to sleep and went out the door for a walk in the cool night air.

Friday evening, Brian showed up with pizzas for them. After dinner, they continued their training with Magic. Anna sat on the steps watching as they repeated their commands, using treats to train the pup. He was learning obedience quickly, although he responded to Nathan's commands best. Magic stared up at the boy with such a love and trust in his brown, soulful eyes, it touched Anna's heart watching them together.

They all settled down in front of the T.V. afterward. Nathan fell asleep curled up to Brian's side and Magic was sleeping on his lap. Anna snuck peeks at them as they watched an old movie.

How had her son and his dog grown attached to this man so quickly? And so had she, she smiled as she admitted it to herself, but was their relationship destined to be platonic, or was there something more there? She was tired of waiting for him to make a move.

When the movie ended, Brian lifted Nathan and Magic up into his arms and put them to bed.

"You want coffee?" Anna asked as they left Nathan's room.

"You bet," he smiled.

Over coffee, Anna had finally worked up her nerve, "why did you never kiss me again?" she asked, blushing. "And why did you run out so fast last week?"

Brian smiled as he leaned forward, staring

deep into her eyes.

"Trust me, I didn't want to leave," his voice was deep and husky. "I just thought it would be best. I know you've been through a lot and I didn't want to push you."

"Oh," Anna was relieved. "I thought maybe you weren't interested. And the way I hear it, you have the girls lining up for a date with you."

Brian laughed softly as he leaned closer, "been checking up on me, have you?"

"No," she exclaimed indignantly, but he cut her off as he crushed his mouth onto hers. His kiss was deeper and more insistent than before. It left them both breathless. Brian took her hand as he stood and pulled her up with him.

"That's why," he whispered as he lightly brushed a wave of hair off her face, her skin tingling from his touch. "I'm afraid I won't be able to stop." He kept her hand in his as he backed away, tracing circles on her palm with his thumb. Anna felt a little dizzy as she stared up at him.

"I'll pick you and Nathan up tomorrow at ten to go to the ranch?" he asked.

She only nodded as she continued staring into his eyes, her thoughts trying to keep up. Then he was gone.

Anna dropped back into her seat at the table. She touched her lips where he had kissed her. She had never known a kiss so electrifying, so intense. She stared at her palm where his thumb had circled. It was still tingling. Why did he run out again, damn him? She thought about following him back to his trailer to confront him, but that sounded more like something Marcie would do.

Brian raced out Anna's door and started walking toward the river behind the trailer park at a steady pace. His whole body was on fire with his need for her and he wasn't sure if he could stop himself from running back inside and ripping the clothes off her beautiful, sexy body.

He slowed his pace and strolled along the river, watching the moonlight play off the slow-moving water. The cool night air quickly brought his senses back under control. He shook his head slowly and grinned as he thought about the startled look he'd seen in her eyes when he kissed her. A look that had quickly caught fire as passion overcame her. He was trying so hard to take it slow and gentle with her, but if she was going to kiss him like that, he knew he was going to lose all control.

Yet, he was afraid of moving too fast and scaring her away. And the one thing he was sure of, he didn't want to lose her.

Was he falling for her? He wasn't sure, he just knew he wanted to spend more time with her.

He sat down by the river, thinking about this amazing woman and wounded child, they had both endured enough pain and sadness for a lifetime. Perhaps it was his and Magic's destiny to bring a little happiness back into their lives.

Chapter 4

Anna didn't know what to wear to the ranch. She settled on jeans and hiking boots. When Brian showed up at ten, she met him at the door with a smile and a hug.

"Wow, what was that for?"

"I'm just happy to see you."

"Me too," Nathan ran and hugged Brian's leg. Anna stepped back to take in Brian's jeans and huge belt buckle and boots. He was wearing a dark blue western shirt that made his eyes seem even more blue than before. A dark brown Stetson cowboy hat completed his look. Dashing, Anna thought. I can't believe he looks even more handsome.

"Guess it's gonna be a good day," Brian

drawled. "You two ready?"

"Yeah," squealed Nathan, "Can Magic come to?"

"Of course, "Brian replied. "My family would love to have him. Brian held the door for Anna as they climbed into his jeep.

"Why's your belt buckle so huge?" Nathan asked.

"I won it," replied Brian. "High school State champion calf roping."

"Do you still do it?" asked Anna.

"Only at the ranch. I enjoy it when it's spring branding, but I lost interest in competing."

"Really?" Anna was surprised. "You must have been pretty good."

"I did o.k. But it's not what I wanna do with my life."

"And firefighting is what you want to do?"

"One of the things. I like helping people," he replied.

"What other things?" she asked.

"I would like to have a ranch of my own

someday. And a family of my own." He looked sideways at her and winked over Nathan's head.

"Mm, sounds nice," she blushed, meeting his gaze for a second, then nervously looking away.

The ranch lay fifteen minutes south of town. Brian pulled into a dirt drive beneath a steel arch that had a circle with a BM in the middle of it. The jeep bumped across a cattle guard and down a winding dirt road. When the house came into view, Anna sucked in her breath. It was a sprawling ranch style house. A porch ran along the entire front of it. We could fit our trailer in there about three times, Anna thought resignedly.

The Chase family came out to meet them. Brian's adoptive father was a tall rancher with weathered skin that was bronze from the sun. He was wearing a white cowboy hat similar to Brian's brown one. His mother was a small framed woman with sandy hair brushed back from her face. Her skin was tanned and weathered from the sun too. Brian introduced them as Ben and Martha.

"Everybody calls me Marty," his mom said as she gave Anna a hug. "Welcome to the ranch."

"Thank you," Anna replied as her gaze traveled over the rolling plains, fat black cattle dotting the landscape here and there. "It's beautiful here."

"The kids are at the arena. Wanna see some horses, Nathan?" Ben asked.

"Yeah," Nathan squealed.

They wandered down a slight hill to a huge oval shaped arena, Magic trailing behind.

Three kids were warming up their horses and three more saddled horses were tied up outside the arena. Brian led them to a big red horse with white stockings halfway up his legs.

"This is Ranger," he said as he untied him. "He's my horse." The big horse put his nose down to Nathan. The little boy wonderingly touched the soft muzzle and giggled as Ranger nuzzled his head.

Magic spied the horses loping around the arena and took off at a dead run.

"No Magic, come back," Anna screamed. The pup was already under the bars of the arena and making a dash for the running horses. He ran straight in front of a galloping horse, barking at it.

The horse was moving too fast to stop.

Anna saw the horse with a young girl on his back leap over Magic. The horse's legs tangled with Magic, knocking the dog to the ground.

Everyone watched in horror as the dog rolled over and over, a tangle of flying hooves and yelping dog. The horse landed past Magic, rear hooves barely clearing him. The pup leapt to his feet and made a beeline back to Nathan, yelping as he ran. He shot under the rails of the fence and leaped into Nathan's arms, knocking the boy over. Anna and Brian checked him over and couldn't find any damage from the dangerous hooves.

"I think he's learned his lesson," Brian

chuckled.

"Let's hope so," Anna's heartbeat hadn't yet returned to normal.

Brian picked Nathan up and set him on the big horse. He instructed Nathan how to hold on as he led Ranger toward the arena.

Anna held her breath, watching. She thought Nathan would be frightened, but he was leaning forward in the saddle instead, rubbing Ranger's neck.

Brian led him around a little, and then climbed up on the horse behind him. He eased Ranger into a trot, then slowly into a lope, Magic running alongside, but at a safe distance.

Nathan's face registered wonder and delight as they ran past Anna. She watched with the older Chase's for a few minutes, then Brian pulled up at the rail.

"You ready to ride, Anna?" She started shaking her head, but Ben was already leading a black mare over to her. At least she's smaller, Anna thought, it won't be so far to fall.

"This here's Tango," Ben said. She's quiet and calm unless you point her at a group of barrels."

"Then you better get ready to tango," he chuckled.

Great, Anna thought as she clumsily climbed up. Let's hope she doesn't see a barrel. She had ridden some with friends in high school, but not for years.

She eased the mare through the gate into the arena and found that Tango responded to the slightest touch of the rein. She kept Tango to a walk as the Chase kids came galloping by her.

Brian took Nathan over to an old gray mare still tied to the rail.

"This will be your horse anytime you can come ride her," he told the boy.

"Her name is Ladybug."

Nathan rubbed her face and neck and the old mare put her head over the boy's shoulder, brought her chin down his back and pulled him closer for a hug. He wound his arms around her neck and buried his face into her chest.

"She likes me," he said in wonder.

"She sure does, sport." Brian sat the boy gently into Ladybug's saddle and led her into the arena. He showed Nathan how to use the reins and then turned them loose. The old horse ambled slowly around the arena. Anna brought Tango alongside her son and they rode together around the arena. The child was overjoyed. He babbled excitedly to her as they rode.

Anna could feel the tension easing out of her muscles. I must have died and gone to heaven, she thought to herself. She was beginning to realize how much she had shrank from the world in the past year. She hadn't taken Nathan out to a movie or a picnic, nothing. It was only work and home for the two of them. Maybe I needed help as much as Nathan, she thought as she rode.

By the time Marty called them in to lunch, Anna and Nathan were feeling comfortable with their horses and having fun together.

They rode back to the barn with Brian and he showed them both how to unsaddle and brush their horses. He got a stepstool from the barn so Nathan could reach the horse's back. Nathan giggled as Ladybug nuzzled his head while he brushed her chest and legs. Magic sat at Ladybug's feet and watched Nathan. If the horse moved a step, the pup moved even faster.

"She loves children," Brian told Anna. "All the foster kids start out with her and work their way up to younger, faster horses."

"Thank you, Brian," Anna said with a tremor in her voice. "This has been amazing." His steel blue gaze locked with hers.

"It's been my pleasure, ma'am." She giggled as he tipped his hat to her.

Chapter 5

Anna met the foster children over lunch. Becky was nine. Chris was twelve and Michael was fifteen.

The family gathered around a big oak dining table, laughing and joking noisily, while Anna and Marty brought the food in from the kitchen.

Lunch was a simple affair of sandwich's and chips, but to Anna and Nathan, it was amazing. They were used to quiet meals in front of the T.V. This noisy bunch was exciting and fun. Nathan joined in their laughter as the children made silly jokes throughout the meal.

Anna gazed around the table at the Chase family and their children. Brian was telling the kids knock-knock jokes, then, when the children said 'who's there?' he would give answers that made no sense. The kids found it hilarious. She couldn't remember the last time she had felt this relaxed and happy.

When lunch was over, they stood on the porch, watching the kids playing with Magic in the yard. Brian told her about the foster kids as he draped his arm lazily over her shoulder.

"Michael came from an abusive family. Chris became a ward of the state when his parents were sent to prison for selling drugs and Becky's mother gave her up last year when she couldn't take care of her any more. They have all three been with my parents less than a year. My dad gives them work to do on the ranch. It keeps them out of trouble and helps them build self-esteem."

"Your parent's seem pretty amazing. I bet they're proud of you."

"Very proud," Marty said as she came up behind them. She dropped down in a wooden porch swing behind them.

"Brian was our first foster child. He was very small when he came to us. We got attached to him so quickly, we decided to adopt him before someone else could. We could never have children of our own, but Brian brought us so much happiness and we thought of him as our own child."

Anna felt overwhelmed by the love she could see and feel from this family. She had never been quite this close to her own family and she was beginning to realize what she'd been missing.

Brian dropped them at the trailer afterward. He had to be back at the fire station for an evening shift.

"I'm leaving it to you to keep up Magic's training," he told her as he held the door of the jeep for her.

"I will," she met his gaze as she stepped out, the intensity she saw in his blue-grey eyes making her feel nervous and excited.

Brian helped Nathan and Magic out of the rear seat and he picked Nathan up for a hug, then kneeled down to hug Magic. The pup jumped on him, licking his face and neck. Anna came in for a hug, too.

"Thank you for today Brian, you don't know what it means to Nathan and I."

"Yeah, I do," Brian drawled as his smile lit up his steel blue eyes. "It was great for me too, Anna."

After he had gone, Anna and Nathan continued Magic's training. The dog already responded to sit, lie down, come, roll over. They were having a little more trouble with 'stay.' He was usually very willing once he understood what was expected of him.

Anna found that she was enjoying working with the dog and watching her son with Magic swelled her heart with pride. He seemed more like a happy, well-adjusted little boy with each passing day. The puppy really was working magic on him.

Brian was back on morning shifts the following week. He came over every evening and he and Nathan continued training Magic.

He brought groceries and helped Anna cook dinner. He also brought Nathan a toy fire truck and a plastic fire helmet much like the one he wore. It said Chief on the front in yellow.

"You look just like our fire chief at the station," Brian told him.
Nathan was so excited, he wouldn't take off his fire hat as he hurried to the sand box with his new truck, Magic trailing happily at his heels.

Yet Brian still seemed to be holding himself back with her, leaving Anna feeling unsure of herself. He gave her a quick kiss every evening when he left, but never offered more. She was beginning to think she should take the initiative and seduce him. If he doesn't make a move soon, I will, she decided. She raced home from work every day to shower and change into something a little sexier than her work clothes. She could see his eyes follow her as she moved about the small kitchen, cooking dinner. She finally decided that if he hadn't made a move by the weekend, then she would.

The hell with these polite cowboys, I'm tired of waiting. She smiled in spite of herself. She actually really liked the gentlemanly, old-fashioned cowboy ways. It made her feel like a lady.

When she was cooking dinner Wednesday evening, Brian pulled a piece of paper from his pocket and put it under a magnet on her refrigerator.

"What's that?" Anna asked.

"Lottery ticket," Brian shrugged his shoulders. "It's no big deal, but if you win you gotta split it with me."

"No problem," she laughed, an edge of sarcasm in her voice. "Don't you know the odds of those things? You have a better chance of being elected president than winning the lottery."

"Ha! Ha!" Brian laughed. "Then maybe I'll be president!"

Nathan came running in to show them Magic's new trick, still wearing his fire chief hat.

"Stay," he held up a hand to Magic as he came into the kitchen carrying a hoola-hoop.

"Go, Magic," he yelled.

Magic ran through the small space and leaped through the hoop. Nathan rewarded him with a dog treat as Anna and Brian clapped their hands and laughed.

"Nice job, Chief," Brian was touched that Nathan never wanted to remove his firemen hat.

Magic was turning into an amazing dog. He seemed happy to do any trick Nathan asked of him. He didn't leave the boy's side until she put them to bed every night, with Magic curled up on his rug beside the bed.

Most mornings she found Magic under the covers, Nathan's arm wrapped around the dog as he slept. She didn't have the heart to reprimand them.

As long as he kept working his magic on her son, she could live with it.

After Nathan and Magic had gone to

bed, with Nathan insisting Brian tuck him in, Brian suddenly took her hand and led her to the couch. She was surprised when he pulled her down on his lap and wound his hands into her long hair, pulling her head down for a kiss. His kiss was insistent as he ran his hands down her back, sending shivers through her. She curled her fingers into his wavy hair and gave herself over to the kiss. She knew there was no stopping this time and damned if she was going to let him run out her door again. He must have sensed her feelings; he picked her up and carried her into her room, still kissing her as he went.

He went with her as he dropped her on the bed, his body moving over hers, never breaking the kiss. He kissed her neck as he slowly undressed her, his hands running from her face down her slender neck and finding her ample breasts, his mouth following where his hands had been. Then, Brian stood up quickly, ripping his clothes from his strong body as he went, dropping

them in a heap on the floor. Anna's eyes
followed his every move, drinking in his
broad shoulders and steel abs. She was in-
trigued by a small patch of dark hair on his
chest. She put her hand up to touch it and he
came down to meet her. Brian made love to
her so gently, so tenderly, she moaned as she
said his name.

Afterward, Anna curled up in his arms,
her head on his broad chest. Her hand found
the hair on his chest again and she drew
circles in it with her fingers.

"I'm sorry Anna," Brian said, his deep
voice husky.
Startled, she pushed herself up onto an
elbow to look at him. "Why are you sorry?"

"I've been trying to be a good boy and
take it slow; I guess I lost my head a little
bit." He didn't actually sound remorseful,
she noted.
Anna laughed. "I could have said stop, you
know?"
Brian chuckled too as he sat up and, grabbing her arms, pulled her down on top of

him.

"Could you?" he asked teasingly as he pulled her down to him and kissed her deeply.

Chapter 6

The next morning at the grocery store, Marcie started in on her again.

"What's up with you, Anna? You look like you're glowing this morning."
Anna smiled at her friend and shrugged her shoulders. "Must be the fresh air," she replied.

"Come on, Anna, be straight with me, are you seeing Brian or not?"

"Yes, I've seen him a few times," Anna answered coyly.
A frown creased Marcie's forehead. "I don't know if that's a good idea, I hear he's a bit of a player. I even went out with him myself once."
"Really? What happened?"

"He bought me dinner, then took me

home. I called him a couple of times, but I guess we just never got around to a second date."

Anna nodded, but didn't say anything. A frown creased her forehead as she thought about it. Was this why Marcie had seemed a little jealous? Marcie finally went back to work, leaving Anna to her thoughts.

In the afternoon, Anna was walking back from the break room in the rear of the store. Marcie was reorganizing the snacks and candy in front of her register.

She had her back to Anna and as she neared, Anna saw her slip a candy bar into her pocket. Anna's forehead creased into a frown. I must be mistaken, she thought. I've been working with her for a year and I've never seen her take anything.

Had she really just seen what she thought she did? Marcie turned and saw her.

"Oh, Hi Anna. I didn't see you there. Hey, would you like to go to a nightclub Friday night. There's a cool club I found in Denver and they have a new band I've been wanting to see."

"No, Sorry, I already have plans."
She hadn't actually made any plans with Brian, but she had no interest in nightclubs in the city.

Anna went back to her register and tried to forget what she'd seen, but it stayed on her mind the rest of day.

Anna had to work the following weekend. She didn't see much of Brian, except for dinner on Sunday. Brian was playing with Nathan and Magic in the yard when she realized she was out of butter.

"Hey Brian, "she called from the open door. "Could I borrow some butter."

"Sure, I'll go get it." He replied from the yard.

"Brian," Anna caught him at her gate. "Can I come with you?"
She saw the slow grin she loved so much etching across his face. It was something between humor and a smirk.

"You wanna see my house?"

"Could I?"

He turned to Nathan, "We'll be right back, stay in the yard with Magic, o.k.?"

"O.K.," Nathan giggled. Anna wasn't sure he would notice they were gone. He was running in circles, Magic nipping at his heels. Brian took her hand and pulled her across the street and through the door of his trailer. Anna sucked in her breath as she went through the door. It wasn't the ratty furniture that caught her attention. Their trailers came furnished and it seemed as if the landlord, Mr. Cranston had hit every yard sale and thrift store in Colorado. It was the boxes stacked everywhere as if Brian had just moved in today.

"Are you kidding me?" She laughed and Brian laughed with her. You've been here, what, three or four weeks now?"

"I've been busy." He said with a grin.

Anna looked around. He had moved the coffee table under the window. There were boxes stacked on it and boxes sitting in front of the couch, acting as a coffee table. Still laughing, Anna ran through the kitchen, opening cabinets as she went. She found paper plates, coffee cups and a coffee pot, but nothing else. She opened his refrigerator. A six pack of beer, one orange, a quart of milk and *thankfully*, a small bowl of butter. She pulled the butter out and carried it with her as she continued her tour. Down the narrow hall she ran, into his bedroom at the end. A bed with a sleeping bag across it, clothes in the closet and boxes everywhere.

"You're pathetic," she laughed as he caught up to her. She headed past him to the bathroom and opened the medicine cabinet. Toothpaste and cologne and nothing else. She playfully took out the cologne, uncapping it and closed her eyes as she inhaled Brian's clean, musky scent. He came up behind her, slid his arms around her waist and kissed her neck. She still had her eyes closed as she leaned back into him, his bottle of cologne still open in her hand. They stood that way for a few minutes, then Brian broke the spell, reminding her of dinner and Nathan.

Her phone was ringing when she got

back to her house. Brian's mother was calling to invite them to lunch at the ranch. Anna was off Monday and Tuesday this week, but Brian had to work.

"Go ahead," he said when she told him about the invite. "It'll be fun for you."

They settled on Tuesday for lunch.

"Bring Nathan and Magic, too." Marty told her.

"Will the other kids be there, too?" Nathan asked when she told him.

"Yes, I think so."

Nathan jumped up and down, clapping his hands.

Tuesday was a bright summer day with a few clouds drifting across an azure sky. The rolling fields of prairie grasses seemed to go on forever as Anna drove her old pickup down the two lane blacktop south of town. It'll be nice to see Marty again, she thought as she drove. She really is a lovely lady.

Nathan was bouncing on the seat with Magic. He was excited to go to the ranch and play with their children.

Marty gave Anna a warm hug when they arrived at the ranch. Chris, Becky and James came out to play with Nathan and Magic.

Anna followed the older woman into the house to help with lunch.

"I couldn't have children," Marty chatted
with her as they cooked. "We took Brian in as a foster child and later adopted him. We enjoyed it so much, we've just kept at it. We still have kids come for a visit after they've returned to their homes, but some, like James, will stay until they are grown. It's so hard to see them leave. It usually helps to take on another child as soon as possible."

"I don't think I could give them up, Marty. You're stronger than I am."

"You're stronger than you think, Anna. You've done a great job with Nathan."

"Thanks Marty, I'm very proud of him and it's so nice to finally see him getting back to normal."

The children laughed and joked with each other over lunch. After the near silence of the past year, the noisy room was music to Anna's ears. She laughed along with them as they made silly jokes.

After lunch, the children sat in the lush green grass in front of the sprawling ranch house while Nathan showed them the tricks Magic had learned. The dog jumped through the hoop, danced on his hind legs as the delighted children clapped and cheered. Anna felt her eyes fill with tears as she watched her son. He was becoming more like himself with each passing day.

The afternoon was over all too soon and Anna and Nathan said their goodbyes, promising to come back soon for more horseback riding.

Nathan chattered excitedly as she drove back toward town. He was so proud of Magic. He was trying to think up new tricks to teach him. He fell silent as a police car came screaming past in their same direction, red and blue lights flashing, siren wailing.

Anna could see a plume of black, ominous-looking smoke over a small hill in the distance. As she approached the hill, she could see more red and blue lights flashing. She slowed her pickup, the hill blocking her view of what was happening. She came to a stop at the top of the hill where a few cars had already stopped in front of her.

Now they could see a tanker truck, flipped on its side off the right shoulder of the road, flames engulfing the entire cab of the truck. A fire truck was pulled alongside it and spraying water onto the scorching flames.

People in the cars in front of her began climbing out for a better look. Anna and Nathan sat in open-mouthed astonishment, speechless.

Just then, a firefighter in full gear came running back toward the cars. His clear face mask muffled his voice. Anna could hear him screaming something, but she couldn't make out the words.

As he neared the people by their cars, his arms waving, she could see people turn and run toward her, terror etching their faces. Now she could hear him.

"Get back," he was screaming, waving his arms at her. Anna felt frozen to her seat.

She couldn't make out his features through the protective fire gear, but the voice, she would know that beautiful deep voice anywhere. Yet, still she sat, frozen. He ran to her truck and pulled Nathan's door open, unbuckled the boy's seatbelt, screaming at Anna as he went, "Get back! The truck is filled with gasoline. It's going to blow." He screamed over the deafening roar of the flames and the chaos of families running past her. He had Nathan in his arms now, Magic had jumped from the truck. Anna felt herself move, but it felt like a dream, the dream where you're trying to run away but your legs just won't move fast enough. It felt like slow motion as she ran down the driver's side of the truck and Brian ran with Nathan down the other side, Magic at his heels. As she ran, thick black smoke rolled across her in waves, obliterating Brian and Nathan.

She felt the explosion before she heard

it, the ground rumbled beneath her feet like an earthquake. Anna was thrown to the ground, her hands scraping against the rough pavement. She pulled herself up and crawled through the smoke, screaming Nathan's name.

She couldn't see anything through the smoke. She felt her way alongside a car and around it, one hand out in front of her, desperately hoping to feel her son's warm body. Anna pulled herself up, using the car for support. "Nathaaan," she screamed over the din of siren's and frightened screams.

As the smoke began to clear, she turned in every direction, frantically searching for her son, her breath coming in short gasps. Her heart almost stopped as she saw a fireman moving through the clearing smoke toward her with a child in his arms and a black dog limping at his heels.

"Oh, Thank God," she breathed as she ran toward them.

"He's o.k.," Brian said as he sat Nathan gently into her arms. She hugged the boy to her, tears streaming down her face.

Brian put his arms around both of them and pulled them to into his broad chest.

"You O.k., Anna?"

"Yes, I'm fine." He could feel her entire body shaking against him.

"You don't seem o.k." He held Nathan with one arm as he put the other around her quivering shoulders.

He turned them away from the fire and over to where a crowd had gathered.

"You two stay here. I've gotta go help with the fire, but I'll be back," he told Nathan as he tousled the boy's hair, then he touched Anna's face lovingly.

Nathan watched Brian in awe as he turned and walked back toward the smoke and flames.

Chapter 7

It seemed like forever before Brian returned.

Anna and Nathan were checked out by E.M.T.'s as they waited. Nathan seemed to be completely fine. Apparently, Brian had moved slower than her with the weight of his fire gear and carrying the child. The blast had knocked them to the ground also, with Nathan under Brian. If not for his protective clothing shielding Nathan, they told her, the child could have been severely burned.

Some of Magic's soft, black hair was singed and his front paws were burned slightly from the hot pavement. The medics wrapped gauze bandages around his paws.

Anna's hands were scraped from the pavement. The medics cleaned and bandaged them. She was still shaking, but not so much as before. Nathan seemed to be taking it all in stride, he was more concerned for Magic than himself.

Once the fire was out, Brian came and found them. He still had on most of his gear, but he had removed his helmet, mask and oxygen tank. He helped them make their way back to her truck. Brian gently pushed her over as Anna climbed behind the wheel. "I'll drive you two home."

From the tone of his voice, Anna knew she shouldn't argue. She slid over and Brian took the wheel. She noticed that the faded blue paint on the hood had bubbled from the intense heat of the fire.

As her shock was fading, Anna was beginning to realize the enormity of what Brian actually did for a living. She looked over at him as he calmly drove them toward home. He had just saved all those families, including her own, from certain death, yet he seemed as calm as if they had been out horseback riding.

He got them home and settled on the

couch, then his friend Jason picked him up and took him back to the scene.

Nathan watched T.V. while Anna started a pot of coffee. The hell with it, she thought as she turned off the coffee pot and grabbed a beer from the fridge. Her hands still trembled slightly as she dropped into a chair at the table and popped the top.

It was dark when Anna heard a soft knock at her door. She had put Nathan and Magic to bed only a few minutes before, and then returned to her seat at the table, still nursing a beer that had long since grown warm. She jumped at the sound, and then moved slowly to the door.

"Hey," Brian's slow smile lit up his face as he held up a six pack of beer.

"Thought you could probably use a beer."

"Sure," Anna smiled too then turned toward her small table. "I had the same thought myself."

"I see." Brian grabbed her before she

could drop back into her chair, pulling her into his strong chest and holding her tight. She buried her head into his chest and she could feel some of the tension leaving her body.

"Hey," Brian took her chin and tilted her head back. "It's going to be o.k. Anna. Everyone's safe now."

She nodded as she felt tears sting her eyes. She pulled away and took a deep breath before her emotions got the better of her.

"I'm o.k. Just still a little shook up, I guess. Let's have that beer."

She pulled two beers from the six- pack he had sat on the table and put the rest in her fridge.

Brian still had a frown of concern on his face as he sat across from her, never taking his eyes off her.

"Nathan seems fine," Anna shifted the conversation as she sipped her fresh beer. "The only thing he's been able to talk about is Brian the superhero, swooping in and saving Magic and him."

Brian smiled and shook his head.

"Just doing my job, ma'am. We superhero's just try to be in the right place at the right time."

Anna could feel her shoulders relaxing as they joked.

"Well, thank you, all the same. Here's to superheroes." She held up her can of beer for a toast. Brian bumped his can into hers, then downed the rest and crumpled the can. They each had another beer as they relaxed, then Brian got up to leave.

"I want to give you guys a chance to rest," he told her as he kissed the top of her head. Anna took his arm before he could turn away.

"Please stay," she looked up to meet his gaze, her eyes imploring him.

Brian didn't answer but picked her up out of her seat and carried her to her room. They crawled into her bed and he wrapped his big arms tightly around her and didn't let go until the sun peeked through her cheap curtains.

Anna took the following day off from work. Her hands were doing fine, she had replaced the bandages with a band-aid on the heel of each hand.

She needed the day to spend with her son more than anything. For the second time in his young life, she realized how close she had come to losing him. She had been absolutely terrified when she couldn't see him through the smoke.

She removed Magic's bandages; his feet were a little tender, but fine otherwise.

It was Nathan she was really worried about. She was afraid the trauma might send him back into the quiet, withdrawn child of the past year.

But he seemed to be over the shock today, and it helped having Magic. Nathan was more concerned for the dog than himself. He talked to Magic constantly, explaining to him in his gentle, childish tone that his paws would be just fine, because Brian had rescued them just in time. Magic stared at the boy intently as he talked, his tail thumping the floor.

Brian came by after work and took them out to dinner. There was only a small café in town, but it was a rare night out for them.
He kept them both laughing throughout dinner, determined to keep their minds off the accident.

He pulled a scrap of paper from his pocket and gave it to Anna. She laughed as she unfolded it. He had bought her another lottery ticket.

"Really, Brian? Are you going to keep wasting money on these things?"

"Yep," his slow smile lit up his steel blue eyes. "I'm a high-stakes gambler."
Anna smiled at him tenderly as he took her hand and held it underneath the table.

"Would you and Nathan like to go to Colorado Springs this coming weekend," he abruptly changed the subject, surprising them. "I'm taking a horse over for my dad on Saturday, if you two would like to ride along?"

"Can we go mom, please?" Nathan

begged.

"Sure honey, it sounds fun." Anna looked at Nathan and smiled. She was excited to go, actually. Anything to spend time with her two favorite guys!

They were laughing and joking when Anna heard her name. She looked around and smiled as Marcie approached their table.

"Hi, Marcie! You know Brian, right?"

"Yes, we've met." Brian's face looked hard as he stood and took Marcie's hand, "good to see you. Would you like to join us?"

"No, thanks, I'm meeting someone." Marcie glanced around and waved at an older man seated at a table in the back.

"I just wanted to say 'hi' and that I'm glad to see things are going well for you two."

She sauntered off to join her friend before they could reply. Brian's face still had a hard, almost angry look.

"She told me you went out with her before," Anna said, thinking maybe he was afraid she'd be upset.

"Yeah, once," he said, then changed the subject.

Anna let the subject drop and forgot about Marcie altogether as Brian kept them laughing throughout dinner.

Brian picked them up Thursday evening for the Fourth of July fireworks show. The fire department held it every year at the high school football field.

They got there early, since Brian was sort of on duty. He had to help set up the fireworks, then he rejoined Nathan and Anna. They had chosen a spot on the grassy field instead of the bleachers. They had brought Magic, but Nathan kept him on his leash. Several passing children stopped to pet him. Nathan demonstrated his and Brian's obedience training as he gave Magic commands to sit, lie down and roll over, while the amused children petted him.

When the show began, the three of them lay back on their blanket. They were so close to the show, Anna could see the firemen lighting the fireworks. Each one was like a sonic boom. They were so close to the action, as each firework exploded in a rainbow of colors, it looked like the sparks were falling toward them. Anna had seen fireworks shows before, but never from right underneath the action. She held her breath as each one fell toward her. She had worried that it might scare Magic, but he looked as awed as she felt. With each boom, he would bark, then the colors danced across his eyes as he watched the sparks falling toward him.

"It looks like the stars are falling down," Nathan said in awe.

"Yeah, it sure does Chief," Brian reached over and tousled the boy's hair.

Anna put her head on Brian's shoulder and hugged Nathan to her side. She couldn't remember when she'd last enjoyed life this much. Certainly not the past year and the years before that, it seemed that she and Nick had spent more time building a life than enjoying life.

Brian took them to the ranch on Saturday morning. Anna closed her eyes and tried not to look as they passed the burned grass where the truck had been.

When they pulled into the ranch yard, Ben led a beautiful bay mare from the corral. Her coloring was dark, with a shiny black mane and tail and a small white star on her forehead. She had intelligent, soft brown eyes.

"She's being donated to a school." Brian told Anna as Ben led the mare into a trailer.

Ben had hooked the trailer up to his truck earlier that morning. They piled in with Magic between them and headed out.

It was a long drive to Colorado Springs. Nathan and Magic fell asleep. Anna curled up to Brian's chest as he moved to put an arm around her.

She watched the countryside fly by out the windows. They were driving through a valley with a river winding through the middle. Cottonwood trees grew tall alongside the river and antelope grazed across the hills.

It was a winding, two-lane road all the way to Colorado Springs and they hardly ever saw another car. It felt like it was just the three of them, crossing the lonely plains, much as the pioneers had done before them. It was a far cry from the noisy city, rush hour traffic and stressful career of her old life. Anna felt as if that had been a dream and this was where she really belonged. She sighed contentedly as she gazed out the window.

The school was actually a small ranch just outside of town. There were stables along one side of a riding ring. The stables faced across the valley, with the eastern hills and desert across the river.

They parked behind the stables and Anna and Nathan wandered toward the ring while Brian went to look for the owner.

There was a crowd of people outside the ring so they kept Magic on a leash. When they arrived at the railing, Anna could see handlers on the ground with their horses, helping small children to mount and leading them around the ring.

A couple with a golden retriever were also watching the children. They walked over to Anna and the dogs sniffed noses, tails wagging. Anna noticed a strange harness on the dog. Like seeing eye dogs have, she thought.

"Hi, I'm Mark and this is my wife Beverly," the stranger said as he held out his hand. Anna shook his hand, then Beverly's.

"That's our daughter, Beth, on the white horse there."

Anna looked at the small blond girl he pointed at.

"This is my son Nathan and his dog Magic."

"Are you enrolling him at the school?" Beverly asked. "This is the best one you'll find for autistic children.

"No, we're delivering a horse. I think she's being donated to the school," Anna answered with a puzzled expression.

Brian came back then with an older lady with salt and pepper hair tied in a bun at the back of her head. She took Anna's hand warmly.

"Hi, I'm Ginger. Are you enjoying our school? It's not a school really, more of a therapy ranch."

"It's amazing," Anna answered. "You help kids with autism?"

"We have blind children that come here to ride, autistic kids, abused children. The horses are therapy animals. We even have a young girl who's paralyzed. She was in a horrible car accident and lost the use of her legs. Her parents told me that she just sat in her room for months after."

"She had given up on life…until they brought her here. Being on the back of a horse gives her back some of the mobility she lost. She's become such a great rider, I've been turning her loose with her handler. The two of them go for long rides across the desert. She says it's like she lost her legs, but grew wings," Ginger said with a smile.

"That's so cool," Anna breathed. She could only imagine it. A young girl no longer able to walk or run, flying across the desert on the back of a horse.

"I would love to do something like this with my life."

"It is very rewarding, and of course, it's also a lot of fun," Ginger replied. "Feel free to come out anytime."

"Thank you," Anna said, still in awe. "I would love to."

Ginger left with Brian to unload the horse and Anna went back to watching the children. She noticed how the children squealed in delight as the handlers led the horses around the ring. Some of them petted the horses constantly and rocked back and forth in the saddle as they rode.

She moved back to stand beside Mark and Beverly at the rail.

"Is your dog a service dog?" she asked Beverly.

"Yes," Beverly turned and smiled, "his name's Sam. We've had him a year. Before we had him, Beth hardly talked to us and when we hugged her, she wouldn't hug us back. It's hard for her to express herself and she's so easily frustrated. Now she laughs and plays with Sam. She's talking to us and giving us hugs. It's like magic, the change he's brought out in her. We take him everywhere with us. Beth has a tendency to wander away, but now she won't let go of his harness when we're out shopping. Sam makes sure she stays with us. He's had some very special training to come this far."

"Did he get that here?"

"No, Ginger is still getting started with therapy horses. It keeps her pretty busy. Sam came from a lady in Denver who trains service dogs for autistic children."

"I would love to do that," Anna's eyes grew wide in awe. "We've only had Magic for a few weeks and he's been so good for Nathan." Anna didn't elaborate on his problems and they all turned back to watching the children on horseback.

"The rocking motion of the horse is calming to Beth," Beverly told her as they watched Beth rocking in her saddle. "And she has a heightened sense of touch, that's why she keeps rubbing its neck. It's been proven that horses are an amazing therapy for children and adults with handicaps."

Anna thought about how much happiness and peace the horses and the ranch had given her and Nathan.

After Brian and Ginger got the new horse settled into her stall, they climbed back into his dad's pickup for the drive home.

Anna was still in awe of Ginger and her therapy school for children. She chattered animatedly to Brian as he drove, Nathan and Magic between them.

"I knew there were such places, but I've never seen one. It would be amazing to work with kids and animals. My family always had a dog when I was growing up and I was a horse-crazy teenager, but I've had less experience with horses. What's the story with the horse we delivered to them?"

"Her name is Rose," Brian answered. "My parents bought her from an auction. Before that, she was at a riding school in Denver. She's been great for the foster kids, but she doesn't like cattle. My parent's need working ranch horses, not just pleasure horses. They can't afford to feed a horse that doesn't earn its keep.

"What about Ladybug, are they gonna get rid of her too?" Nathan sounded so upset, Brian reached over and hugged the boy to him.

"No, Chief, Ladybug has worked on the ranch for a long time, she's retired from ranching, but my folks won't ever sell her."

"Oh, O.K." Nathan breathed a sigh of relief, then curled up to Brian's side.
Brian wrapped his big arm tenderly around the boy.

"What do you mean, Rose doesn't like cattle?" Anna questioned.

"Animals are like people in that way, some racehorses don't like racing, there are jumpers that don't like jumping." Brian explained.

"Rose doesn't like working cattle, but she loves working with kids. But when you do find something they enjoy, they're usually unstoppable," he continued.

"A cutting horse or roping horse is usually much like an Olympic athlete. They train really hard to do something they enjoy."

Anna grew quiet as she thought about the therapy ranch for the rest of their return drive, the empty horse trailer bouncing and rattling behind them.

When they returned the truck and trailer to the ranch, Marty and Ben invited them to come back the following day for a family horseback ride and picnic. Nathan was excited, "Can I ride Ladybug again, please mom?" Anna looked questioningly at Brian.

"Sounds like fun," his slow grin was creasing his face.

"Great, I'll pack a lunch for us." Marty gave Anna a hug, then hugged Nathan before heading back into the house.

Anna started dinner when they got back to her trailer, while Brian and Nathan watched T.V.

She had her back to them, working at the

stove when she felt strong arms circle her waist. She turned to find Brian towering over her.

"Sit down, it's my turn to cook." She looked at him to see if he was joking.

"I cook better than you anyway," he joked. He grabbed a beer for her and one for himself, sat her down at the table and took over dinner. Anna had been about to put chicken breasts in the oven.

Brian made a homemade barbeque sauce, brushed it over the chicken, then added beer to the pan and popped it in the oven while he made a salad.

Anna and Nathan were impressed with dinner. It was simple, yet delicious.

"This chicken is amazing, I'll have to let you cook more often," Anna hinted.

"Anytime," Brian replied with a smile. "I actually really enjoy cooking and trying new recipes."

"Is it going to make me drunk?" Nathan had seen Brian adding beer to the pan.

"No Chief, it only adds flavor." Brian

laughed as the boy munched away happily, his face smeared with barbeque sauce.

They lay in bed together later that night, her head on his shoulder. His lovemaking was still the sweetest, most tender she had ever known, yet with so much intensity. It was like nothing she had ever experienced.

"I could see myself running a place like that," she murmured against his chest.

"Like what?" his voice sounded huskier than usual.

"The ranch for kids, I would love to do something like that. Only my ranch would have dogs and horses and goats…" her voice trailed off as she yawned. She could feel her eyes closing against her will.

He chuckled, she could hear the rumble through his chest.

"Sounds nice." He trailed his fingers up and down her arm, thinking about her ranch, smiling in the dark.

"I love you," she mumbled against his chest.

He wasn't sure he heard her correctly.

"What was that?" he bent his head so he could see her face. Her eyes were closed and her breathing was slow and even.

"I love you, too." he whispered as he kissed the top of her head.

Chapter 8

Sunday dawned bright and clear, a slight prairie wind blowing, promising slightly cooler temperatures if the breeze held.

Anna woke still held tight by Brian's strong arms. She opened her eyes to find him staring down at her.

"I love you too, Anna. I've wanted to tell you that for a while, but I was a little scared, I guess. I'm glad you said it first."

"What? But I only thought it, I didn't say it." She sat up in bed quickly, her face turning different shades of red as she realized what she'd just said. Brian reached for her and pulled her gently back down beside him.

"It's o.k., Anna." He hugged her to his broad chest.

"I love you too, baby" he murmured into

her hair. "And, I love Nathan and Magic too."

Anna stayed quietly folded in his arms as she let the warmth of his words wash over her. She had thought she would never be able to find love again after losing her husband. In fact, she had done just the opposite and avoided any chance of falling in love. Had she been hiding as much as mourning? And how had this beautiful man come into her life and stolen her heart before she had even realized it?

When they arrived at the ranch, Brian made Anna brush and saddle Tango while he helped Nathan with Ladybug.

Ladybug put her head over Nathan's shoulder for her customary hug as he brushed her chest and neck. The boy was literally trapped by the horse until she lifted her head. He wrapped his arms around her neck and returned the hug as he giggled.

The Chase family was already saddled up and waiting for them. Anna thanked them again for the invitation. It was nice getting back on a horse after all the years she'd spent away from it.

Brian quickly saddled Ranger while Anna was still trying to figure out what goes where. Brian led Ranger over to her and showed her what to do, and then he helped Nathan up onto Ladybug.

They set off across the ranch at a sedate pace, Ben leading the way on his paint gelding. They rode south across the rolling plains about two miles, chatting as they rode. Magic trailed along behind, careful of the horses feet.

Anna told Marty about the children's ranch and how much she would love to do something like that.

"It's a lot of work, but it would be very rewarding," Marty told her.

"I bet there are even more things I could do," Anna said thoughtfully. "What about training dogs like Magic to work with children?"

"I know dogs are used for therapy in a lot of places these days. Maybe it would be a good place to start."

Anna rode quietly for a bit, rubbing Tango's shiny black neck as ideas raced through her mind.

They rode into a green valley, scattered cottonwoods shading a fast running stream. It looks like a scene from a postcard, Anna thought to herself as they dismounted.

Brian showed them how to drop the reins to ground tie their horses.

"All ranch horses are taught to ground tie," he explained, "there's not always a tree or fence post out on the plains and it would be a long walk back to the barn."

Nathan dropped Ladybug's reins to the ground, and then put up his hand as he backed away.

"Stay," he commanded. Ladybug stared at him with her big doe eyes as he backed away. Magic sat down beside Ladybug, his tail wagging, as Nathan backed away. He wouldn't move until Nathan finally called to him.

"Good boy, Magic," he said as he rubbed Magic's ears, "but I was actually talking to Ladybug."

Marty began unpacking food from their saddlebags while the children ran to play in the stream. She laid a yellow blanket on the grass, then unpacked sandwiches and sodas for everyone.

Brian sat down in the grass beside Anna and draped his arm over her shoulder as they watched the children splashing in the stream with Magic. The kids were standing knee-deep in the stream, throwing sticks into the water for Magic to fetch.

Anna looked around at the gently rolling hills, the group of ranch horses standing off to the side, reins trailing, and then her gaze traveled over Brian and his family, then finally to Nathan splashing and laughing in the water.

"It just doesn't get any better than this," she said with a deep sigh of contentment as she leaned her head on Brian's shoulder. She thought of her old life, the daily stress and noise of the city. It felt so far away from the quiet beauty of this ranch.

"You got that right, babe." Brian couldn't think of a time in his life when he had been this happy.

They stayed there for a while, enjoying the view and the children, until Marty called everyone over for lunch.

The family relaxed in the grass another hour after lunch, enjoying the peace of the country-side. Anna and Brian splashed in the stream with the children and threw sticks for Magic.

Finally, they repacked the saddlebags and mounted up for the two mile trek back to the house.

As they passed the arena, Anna saw three red barrels placed in a triangle pattern across the ring.

Before she could stop her, Tango turned through the gate of the arena.

"Whoa, Tango," Anna yelled as she pulled on the reins. She didn't stop so Anna turned her in a circle to the right. Little did she know that's what barrel racers do to get there horse lined up on the first barrel. Tango spun to the right and shot forward so fast, Anna had to grab the saddle horn to stay on. Tango rounded the first barrel at a fast gallop and stretched out for the second one. She rounded it to the left and Anna felt like her knee was going to brush the ground, the horse was leaning so far into the turn.

She had lost one stirrup when Tango leaned so far but she had a death grip on the saddle horn.

Tango ran so fast toward the third barrel, Anna felt as if she were flying. The horse slowed slightly around the barrel, but Anna still lost her other stirrup and she gripped her legs tight around the horse. As Tango rounded the last barrel, Anna could feel her powerful hindquarters bunch as she almost leapt off the ground. She galloped so fast back down the arena and through the open gate, Anna's eyes stung from the wind.

Tango slowed and Anna turned her around to see the Chase family and Brian watching her in open-mouthed astonishment. Her entire body was trembling with adrenaline as she rejoined the others.

"I didn't know you were a barrel racer," Brian was looking at her as if he had just met her.

"I'm not, Tango is." Anna laughed nervously. "I've never done that before."

"Were you scared, Mommy?" Nathan asked worriedly.

"No, Sweetie, it was fun, actually."

"Told you, "ya better be ready to Tango," Brian's father had a sparkle in his eyes as he laughed with her.

"I hope you all enjoyed the show," Anna said, still laughing. "I certainly did, it was quite a rush."

"I've been learning to barrel race," Becky rode alongside her, "would you like to learn with me?"

"Sounds great, but maybe I need a slower horse to start out with," Anna said as she patted Tango's neck. Tango tossed her shiny black head, obviously proud of herself.

Chapter 9

Anna picked Nathan up from Mrs. Wilson's Monday after work and took him to the library.

She had decided to do some research on therapy animals and she didn't have a computer at home. She let Nathan browse the children's books while she went online.

She was engrossed in her research when she felt a hand on her shoulder. She looked up to find Marcie standing behind her.

"Whatcha reading?" Marcie was trying to read over her shoulder so Anna quickly closed the page she had been reading.

"Just doing a little research. What've you been up to? I haven't seen much of you lately, except for work. I've missed hanging out with you.

"Yeah, I've been pretty busy. I've been going to Denver with a couple of friends, hitting the clubs, stuff like that. I figured you were too busy to hang out, you know, since you've been seeing Brian."

"Don't be silly, Marcie, you know I'll always make time for you. Hey, why don't you come over for dinner sometime. We would love to have you."

"Do you mean we, as in Brian and I, or Nathan and I?"

"Well, if it makes a difference, Brian is on evening shift this week, so, if you would rather, we could do it this week. Do you have a problem with Brian?"

"No," Marcie hesitated, "I told you he's kind of a player, right?" Anna nodded, not sure where this was going.

"I just don't want to see you get hurt, that's all." Marcie squeezed her shoulder.

"What do you mean, he's kind of a player?" Anna frowned. Of all the words she could think of to describe Brian, player was definitely not one of them.

"He dated a lot before you, I would see

him at the clubs. Like I told you, I even went out with him once."

"And?" Anna waited.

"And nothing. At least as far as I was concerned. He didn't ask me out again or return my calls. Next thing I hear, he's going out with you."

"Oh," Anna wasn't sure what to think. She didn't have that much experience with dating, but it didn't sound like such a big deal to her.

Nathan interrupted her thoughts to show her the books he'd picked out. Marcie gave a smile and a wave and moved on through the romance section of books. Anna looked at the books Nathan had chosen, and then went back to her research as he sat on the floor, flipping through a book.

Marcie came for dinner on Wednesday. Anna was chatting with Marcie while she cooked and Nathan played with Magic in the yard.

Brian stopped by on his break and

Marcie seemed to scowl as he walked in. Her face changed as Brian smiled politely and shook her hand, she giggled and seemed positively flirty with him.

Anna saw Marcie's eyes travel down his body, then slowly back up to his face. Brian turned his back on her as he moved over to Anna.

"I just came by to drop off your weekly winner," he joked as he stuck a new lottery ticket on the refrigerator, replacing the previous week's losing ticket.

"Really?" Marcie was aghast. "Why are you wasting your money on those things? You don't really think you're going to win, do you?"

"No," Brian smiled at her. "I think Anna's going to win, it's her ticket.

Marcie scowled at him. Anna could feel the tension between the two of them.

"Well, I've gotta get back to work." He gave Anna a hug and a quick kiss. "It was good to see you again, Marcie," he said politely.

When he was gone, Marcie started with

the questions.

"Is it serious with you two? Have you slept with him yet?"

Anna had never been one to discuss her private life. She dodged the questions as best she could, then changed the subject.

Dinner was a little quiet compared to the past. Marcie seemed a little cold and still not very happy about Anna and Brian.

Anna really couldn't understand it. Marcie had been a friend to her over the past year, but their relationship had never been overly close, since Anna wouldn't go to the clubs with her.

Is she jealous? Anna wondered. It doesn't make much sense, there doesn't seem to be any love lost between those two. She shook it off and quickly forgot all about. Marcie didn't stay long after dinner. She chatted with Anna for a bit over coffee, and then said she had a bit of headache.

"Maybe we can get together again soon," she told Anna as she rose to leave. "I'll buy you guys dinner at the café next time."

"Sure, sounds like fun." Anna replied as she walked her to the door.

After Marcie left, Anna followed Nathan outside to help with Magic's training. She sat down on the steps as Nathan called Magic to him.

"Sit, Magic." Nathan pointed his finger at the dog and Magic sat down obediently.

"Stay," he put his hand up, palm out toward Magic as he backed away.
Magic stared happily at the boy, his tongue lolling as he obeyed the commands.

"Good boy, Magic." Nathan handed him a dog treat, then put his hand out, palm down.

"Down," he ordered.
Magic lay down as instructed, and then Nathan circled his hand in the air.

"Roll over." Magic rolled onto his back, feet in the air as Nathan rubbed his tummy.

"Now you try, Mommy."

"O.k., Sweetie."
Anna repeated the same commands as Nathan had, making sure to use the same

hand signals.

They were getting to a point where Magic would respond with only hand signals. Magic seemed to enjoy the training as much as they did.

"Let's try a new one," she told Nathan. She had Magic sit first, then said, 'shake.' She picked up his paw and shook it, then gave him a dog treat. They repeated it several times until Magic began lifting his paw when they told him, 'shake.'

"Very good, Magic," she rubbed his head. "We should stop for today, though. We don't want to overdo it."

"O.K. Mom."

Nathan picked up a dog toy and Magic chased him around the yard, trying to get it away from him. Anna sat back on the steps and watched the two of them, contentment enveloping her as she realized how much this sweet black dog had changed their hollow lives.

The following day, she picked Nathan

up from Mrs. Wilson's as usual after work, and then realized she'd left her house keys at work.

As she drove with Nathan and Magic back to the store, she saw Marcie's car at the fire station, parked beside Brian's jeep. How odd, she thought as she drove. Marcie's not making much sense these days. She retrieved her keys from the store and headed for home.

As she passed the fire station again, she saw Marcie's car still parked beside Brian's.

When Brian stopped by on his break, he didn't mention Marcie, so Anna didn't bring it up either.

Brian had time to stay for dinner before going back to work. Anna told him over dinner about her research on therapy dogs.

"I think if we could get Magic certified as a therapy dog, we could take him to visit hospitals and retirement homes." Anna said.

"They don't get to keep him, do they?" Nathan looked alarmed.

"No sweetie, just a visit. You could come too if you like. We could both be his handlers."

"Okay," Nathan still wasn't sure what it meant, but as long as he got to spend time with Magic, it was o.k. by him.

"Sounds like it'll be fun. It'll give you two a hobby to do together," Brian said.

"You have to come too, you are one of his trainers," Anna locked eyes with Brian, his steel blue gaze still made her knees weak.

"Sure, if it's what you both want."

"Yeah, Brian, you have to come with us," Nathan said excitedly.

"O.k. Chief, you got it," Brian tousled the boy's head. Magic put his shiny, black head in Nathan's lap, his tail wagging furiously. He didn't want to be left out.

Friday, Anna was restocking the Pharmacy section at work. She had a cart with new shampoo's and makeup that had been delivered that morning. She was reorganizing shelves to make room for it when a customer asked for help finding vitamins. She showed the elderly man where the vitamins were on the next aisle. As she came back around to her boxes, she saw Marcie walking by her cart, going toward her register. Marcie didn't see Anna behind her. As she passed the boxes, Anna saw her take a lipstick from a box and drop it in her pocket without ever slowing her stride. *O.k., I know I didn't imagine that,* Anna wasn't sure what she should do. Marcie was her friend, yet she felt a loyalty to Mr. Jones for her job.

When so many people were out of work, she was grateful to be working at all. She couldn't believe Marcie would risk her job for a tube of lipstick.

She ran into Mr. Jones later in the break room.

"Mr. Jones, I was wondering if this store has video cameras?

"Sure does," Mr. Jones said with a note of pride in his voice. "Just had them installed last year."

"Do you watch the videos?" Anna hedged.

"Only if there's something missing. Why, is something missing?"

"Well," Anna paused, and then said, "I was putting away the new lipsticks and the invoice said twenty, but I only had nineteen in the box."

"Oh, that happens," Mr. Jones smiled kindly at her. "We just mark it off our inventory and let the factory know they shorted us one." He scratched his head.

"Although, now that you mention it, it has been happening a lot lately." He saw her worried expression. "But don't worry about it, we'll take care of it." He wandered away, still scratching his head.

The following day was Saturday, her weekend off and Brian took Anna, Nathan and Magic to the ranch for another picnic. He told them it would be just the three of them, since the Chase family had gone into Denver for the day.

Anna steered Tango away from the arena as they passed. She wasn't sure her heart could take another wild ride just yet.

Magic loped alongside Ladybug, always keeping Nathan in his sights. The boy and dog had become inseparable. Nathan was still working on new tricks and Magic had an uncanny ability for learning. They both really seemed to enjoy the training.

As they rode, Brian kept urging his horse faster and faster. Nathan and Anna were having trouble keeping up. Both their horses broke into a trot to keep up with Ranger.

Anna glanced at Nathan to see how he was handling it. The boy was smiling and urging Ladybug faster. Finally their horses had to lope to catch Brian. As they caught up to him, Brian looked at first Anna, then Nathan. Seeing they were o.k., he let Ranger out into a gallop.

As they raced across the fields, they were laughing and shouting. Brian pulled up by the stream as Anna and Nathan came racing up to him, red-faced and laughing.

They all hopped down, ground-hitching their horses and Brian unpacked his saddlebags. Anna grabbed a soda from him, opened the bottle and screeched as soda flew over her.

Brian and Nathan had a good laugh as she went to the stream to wash off. She hadn't thought about their wild gallop shaking up the sodas!

After sandwiches and cheese and crackers, she settled down beside Brian to watch Nathan and Magic play in the stream.

When Brian draped his arm over her shoulder, Anna turned to look up at him and he kissed her neck playfully.

"Thank you, Brian." She looked into those steel blue eyes she loved so much.

"For what?"

"Everything. You've brought my son back to me. You've given both of us a life again."

"You have to thank Magic for some of it." Brian seemed a little embarrassed.

"I will. But without you, we wouldn't have him either."

"I didn't have that much of a life before

either, you know. I didn't have anyone special in it." He kissed her lips gently.

Just then, Anna squealed as they both got sprayed with water. Magic and Nathan had come running over, Magic stopping in front of them to shake water from his coat, Nathan jumped on Brian, soaking wet and wrestled him to the ground. They laughed and wrestled in the grass until it was time to head back.

Anna felt so much at peace with the world as they rode slowly back to the barn. She was amazed how relaxing and enjoyable a simple horseback ride and picnic could be.

She watched Brian in front of her as she rode. He sat tall in his saddle, his cowboy hat pulled down at a rakish angle over his face.

Yep, still looks like a movie star, she smiled to herself.

Later, lying in bed with her head on his shoulder, Brian asked her again about training Magic as a therapy dog.

"There's a two day training session in Denver next week if you can get the days off," he told her.

"Which days?" she asked, lazily trailing her fingers through the hair on his chest.

"Tuesday and Wednesday."

"I have Monday and Tuesday off next week, but maybe I can switch with Marcie."

"What about you? Are you coming too?"

"Nope, sorry, gotta work. I would ask, but we've been shorthanded."

"That's o.k., she said sleepily. I'll take Nathan anyway if I can get free,"

"What would you do if you won the lottery?" he asked unexpectedly.

"I don't know. I think I would like a ranch like your parents have, and it would be great to do something like the children's ranch we went to. Why, did you win?"

"No, I was just wondering. It's not like you would know if you won anyway. You hardly ever check your ticket."

"I know, I'm horrible! I always try to grab it off the fridge, but I'm usually racing out the door. Anyway, Nick and I had money and I can tell you, it doesn't buy happiness. We spent so much time looking for the perfect house, the perfect furniture, the best cars. And now, I have a rental trailer with ratty furniture, but I've realized it doesn't matter. I have Nathan and you and Magic. Nothing else will ever compare, not the richest house or the finest cars."

"I love you, Anna. It's nice to know you're not after my money," he joked as he held her.

Brian invited Anna to go out on a real date on Friday night.

He had already set up a sleepover for Nathan with Brenda's kids if Anna was in agreement.

She hadn't really given it any thought until he mentioned it; they had been so busy horseback riding and training Magic, but she had never been out on a date with Brian, just the two of them.

Nathan was delighted. It was his first real sleepover with friends. Anna dropped him off early on Friday afternoon, thanked

Brenda profusely, and then raced home to get ready.

She took a hot bath and shaved her legs, then tore through her closet like a whirlwind.

Most of her best clothes were business suits she'd worn as a realtor. She went through every outfit, then finally pulled out a red knee-length skirt. It had a matching red jacket, but she returned it to the hanger. She found a white gauzy button-up blouse with three-quarter length sleeves. She tried it on with the red skirt, then opened an extra button on the blouse.

"There," she told her reflection in the full-length mirror. "Sexy, not slutty," she giggled to herself as she redid the button. She found a decent pair of black pumps, not the sexy heels she would have preferred, but they would have to do. Her legs were golden tan from her summer spent outdoors so she did without the pantyhose.

Brian arrived promptly at six, just as he'd promised. He whistled when she answered the door and Anna blushed like a schoolgirl. She hadn't felt like this since her senior prom.

Brian was quite the dashing figure himself in a pair of new jeans and cowboy boots, a dark brown western cut blazer and his dark brown cowboy hat.

She told him as much as he leaned in and kissed her. Anna closed her eyes as she inhaled the musky scent of his cologne. Brian took her hand and led her out to his jeep, holding the door for her as she stepped inside.

He drove north out of town and she looked at him quizzically.

"Are we going into Denver?" She thought maybe he was taking her downtown. It was full of fine restaurants, nightclubs and famous micro-breweries. She knew it would be a lot of fun, but it held too many memories for her. She'd been there much too often with her husband in years past.

Brian only looked at her and smiled mysteriously. He turned his jeep off onto a dirt road before crossing the river and followed the dirt track downriver.

Now, she was really mystified. He seemed to be taking her to the middle of nowhere. The small dirt road paralleled the river for about two miles, then Brian pulled off the road and the jeep bounced across the grass.

He parked under huge cottonwood trees that formed a shady canopy over the jeep.

Brian came around and held her door, taking her hand and helping her from the jeep.

Then he opened the back window on his jeep and pulled out a covered picnic basket. Anna laughed nervously. "We got all dressed up for a picnic?"

Brian only gave her his slow mysterious smile again, then took her hand and led her through the trees.

"Clearly the wrong choice of shoes," she giggled as her heels sank into the sandy soil. They reached the edge of the river and her breath caught and she stood frozen, taking in The scene. The river was held back by boulders and rocks causing it to form a small waterfall at this spot he'd so carefully chosen. There was a deep pool at the base of the falls, then it cascaded across river stones, making a beautiful sight and sound.

Brian had obviously been here already, there was a blanket spread under the trees, with luminarias, brown paper bags filled with sand and each holding a single candle, placed in a square surrounding the blanket.

There were small lanterns hanging from the lower limbs of the trees. Brian went to each one and flipped a switch and a battery-operated candle came to life, flickering realistically.

"We want to practice fire safety, right?" he smiled at her as he worked.

Anna could only smile and nod as she stood looking around, stunned. She couldn't believe he'd gone to all this trouble just for her.

The setting sun didn't reach underneath the huge cottonwoods and Brian took a long lighter, the kind used for charcoal grills, and began lighting each candle in the paper bags.

Next, he came over to her, took her hand and led her over to the blanket.

They both sat down in the middle of the blanket, surrounded by the warm glow of candles.

The ground was deep sand alongside the river. It made for a very comfortable seat on the blanket. Anna kicked off her shoes and tucked her legs under her, leaning her weight on her hand. Her long honey-brown hair nearly brushed the blanket as she watched Brian contentedly.

Brian opened his picnic basket and removed a bottle of wine, crackers, cheeses and deli meats. He'd even brought plastic wine glasses and he poured them each a glass. They nibbled the cheese and crackers as the darkness closed in around them. Crickets and night birds were starting up their songs and the small waterfall added its own special tune.

Brian held his wineglass up to hers, "here's to you, Anna."

"No, to us," she stared into his intense

grey-blue gaze as they clinked their plastic glasses together.

Anna watched the way the flickering orange candlelight played off his face and made his eyes sparkle. She couldn't get enough of his beautiful face as she held his stare. She felt lucky that this gorgeous, loving man who could probably have any girl he wanted, would want to be here with her.

Finally, Brian broke the stare and, taking her wineglass from her hand, he sat both glasses down in the sand, took off his cowboy hat and kissed her hungrily.

He pushed her down on the blanket and made love to her slowly, as the moon rose through the trees, casting a silvery light on their naked bodies as the crickets continued their serenade.

Chapter 10

Brian took them fishing in the river behind the trailer park on Sunday. He let Nathan use a fishing pole of his, with the promise to buy him one next time they went to town. He showed the boy how to bait his hook and how to cast his lure. After a few tries, Nathan was getting the hang of it.

Magic sat on the bank watching, looking as if he'd like to follow the lure into the river each time they cast.

Anna sat in the sand and soaked up the sun. She had a fishing pole in front of her, but she didn't really care about fishing. She was enjoying the peacefulness of the river and watching Brian and Nathan having fun together. She watched Brian as he helped Nathan cast his pole. The muscles in his back and shoulders rippled as he moved. His sandy hair curled just over his collar, peeking out from under his ever-present, dark brown cowboy hat. She still felt as if she were floating after their date the other night. Never had she known a sweeter, more romantic man. He'd made her feel like a princess.

Brian must have felt her stare, he turned his head and looked her up and down with fire in his eyes, his slow grin spreading across his face.

Anna and Nathan took Magic in to Denver the following week to the training seminar. There were only three other dogs and their handlers getting their therapy dog certificates. Each handler and dog team had to prove to the tester that their dog could walk quietly on a leash, obey commands, interact calmly with other dogs and strangers. Magic went through the test with ease. He loved nothing more than being the center of attention. Anna and Nathan enjoyed themselves too. Anna explained to

Nathan how they could take Magic for visits to hospitals and other facilities. "It'll be a fun hobby for us and Magic," she told him.

After the seminar, they found a hotel in Denver that accepted pets. They had to take Magic back the following morning for his veterinarian exam. The dogs had to pass a clean bill of health before they could be certified 'therapy animals.'

Anna ordered pizza and sodas for them, then she called Brian at work to tell him how well Magic had done.

"I knew he would," she could hear the pride in Brian's voice. "He was trained by the best!"

"Hey, I helped, too." Anna chided.

"O.k., it was a team effort. I'm glad he did well. I wanna go on his first visit, too."

"I was thinking of the retirement home in Carson. Mrs. Wilson has told me over and over again how happy Magic has made her. I think he will enjoy the elderly."

"You got it, babe."

Brian went on to tell her about his day. "Someone must have thrown a cigarette out a car window south of town. It only took us an hour to get the fire out, but if the winds had changed direction and pushed the flames toward town, we would have been in trouble."

"I'm glad you got it out," Anna was thinking of the small hospital that sits just on the south edge of town when she heard a knock on the door. "Must be the pizza. I better run."

"O.k., I love you."

"Love you too," she hung up and ran for the door.

It was a rare night out for Nathan and Anna. They ate pizza and watched T.V., staying up too late, without a care in the world. It was such a nice mother and son evening, Anna decided they should do it more often.

The next morning, Magic passed his vet exam and was given his therapy dog tags for his collar and a blue vest that identified him as a therapy dog.

His certificate would come in the mail, they were told.

Nathan wanted Magic to wear his vest as they drove back to Carson. It really does look nice, Anna thought as she scratched his head while she drove. *Royal blue against his shiny black hair.* She was looking forward to Magic becoming a *working dog.*

They decided to stop and do some shopping on the way home; Nathan needed new jeans and Carson was pretty limited for clothing stores. They found several pairs of jeans and new shirts for Nathan and Anna bought herself a new red blouse and a pair of cowboy boots.

Now, at least I'll have proper boots when we go riding, she thought proudly. Nathan begged her for cowboy boots, too.

"I want a pair just like Brian's," he told her. She found a pair his size and a small white cowboy hat.

She was barely going to have enough left for rent this month, but the smile on

Nathan's face made it worth it. He didn't want to take his boots off after he tried them on; Anna had to remove the tag so the cashier could ring them up.

"I can't wait to show Brian," Nathan chattered as they left the store.

The shopping had taken longer than she planned and she was in a hurry as she pulled her truck into the trailer park. She had promised Brian dinner when she got back and she had to admit, she had missed him. He had become such a part of their lives, it didn't seem right without him.

She was shocked to see Marcie's car parked beside Brian's jeep at his trailer. Now she had to know what was going on!

They took their packages into the house and Anna started a pot of coffee before she sat down to wait for Brian. She noticed her hand was shaking as she reached for the coffeepot.

It's probably nothing, she kept telling herself, but she had a really bad feeling. When a knock sounded at the door, Anna took a deep breath and opened it. It was Marcie instead of Brian on her step.

"Can I talk to you in private for a minute?" Marcie asked.

Anna looked over at Nathan and Magic curled together on the couch watching T.V. She stepped outside and closed the door. She crossed her arms and waited for Marcie to speak.

"I got fired today." Marcie said angrily. "I know you saw me take the lipstick and I know you got me fired."

Anna's mouth dropped open, her arms dropped to her sides, but she remained speechless.

"Well, I got you back," Marcie continued. "I just came from sleeping with your boyfriend. I told you he was a player." Anna still hadn't said a word as Marcie whirled and stomped over to her car. She backed out of Brian's drive, raced the engine and squealed her tires as she tore out of the trailer park.

Anna was still standing in the same spot,

her face white as a sheet, when Brian walked up to her.

"Did she tell you?"

Anna couldn't believe he was so nonchalant. "Yeah, she told me she thinks I got her fired and she paid me back."

"What do you mean, she paid you back?"

"Really Brian, did you really think it wouldn't bother me if you sleep with my friend? Or at least what I thought was a friend."

"Sleep with her? I didn't sleep with her. She came on to me, but I pushed her away. She said she wanted to be the one to come over and tell you that and apologize to you."

"Sure, Brian, then what was she doing there in the first place? And I saw her car the other day at the fire station, too." Without waiting for his answer, Anna turned, went inside and quietly closed the door on him.

Brian watched the door close in his face, too dumbfounded to speak. He finally turned and walked slowly across the street to his own trailer, his mind a whirlwind of confusion. He paced back and forth through the trailer. The more he paced, the angrier he became. He went out the door, jumped in his jeep and started the engine. He was going to find Marcie, drag her back if he had to and force her to tell Anna the truth. He sat there, unmoving for a few minutes, then turned off the engine and walked back inside. He was much too angry to confront Marcie. But why would she do this to us? He went back to his pacing, trying to make sense of the whole thing. There had to be a way to convince Anna he was telling the truth. He finally stopped his pacing, grabbed a beer from the fridge and sat down on the couch, his mind still racing.

Chapter 11

Anna made a quick dinner for Nathan, she told him she wasn't hungry and she had a headache, then she went and laid across her bed as Nathan went back to the T.V. She laid there, staring at the ceiling until Nathan came in to check on her.

She forced herself up, helped Nathan into his pajamas and tucked him into bed. Then she went back and dropped across her bed again. She never got undressed, never got under the covers, just kept staring at the stained ceiling of her small room. *How dare he do this to us?* She knew how much this was going to hurt her little boy too. *Hasn't he already been through enough?*

Sometime in the night she felt Magic

jump onto the bed. When he curled up beside her, Anna turned over on her side, put an arm around the dog and pulled him to her. She finally got a little sleep, holding Magic against her like a child's worn out teddy bear.

When Anna dropped Nathan at Mrs. Wilson's the next morning, she forced herself not to look at the shiny black jeep across the street. Mrs. Wilson asked if she was feeling alright, she looked so haggard and pale.

"I'm fine," she lied. "Just a bit of a headache."

When she got to the store, Jeannie was abuzz with the news of Marcie being fired. Customers even asked her about it. I guess it's true, she thought, there are no secrets in a small town. She somehow made it through the day, ringing up customers and bagging groceries on auto pilot. It wasn't that her mind was somewhere else, it was turned off completely. She drove home in the same state. She performed the functions of driving, but she couldn't have described anything she saw.

She picked Nathan and Magic up and when she went to unlock her door, she saw an envelope tucked into it. She pulled it out and stuck it in her pocket as she walked in, never looking at the trailer across the street. She went to take a hot bath while Nathan and Magic played in the yard. She eased into the tub of hot water, and then pulled the letter from her jeans on the floor. She ripped the envelope and pulled the letter out. A slip of paper was folded inside the letter. She unfolded it first and saw it was a lottery ticket. She felt like her heart was going to break right out of her chest. A lottery ticket, so typical Brian, she thought. She read the note slowly, not sure if she should just toss it without reading it.

Anna,

I think I was set up, for what reason, I'm not sure. I took Marcie out on one date last year. She came onto me then and I rejected her.

I think she's hated me ever since. She stopped by the fire station a few days ago with a broken smoke detector.

I couldn't fix it, but I told her I have a couple new ones at my place. She stopped by for them and came on to me again. She said she wanted to tell you she came on to me and apologize to you, which I guess was a lie. I don't understand the rest of it, about you getting her fired. I hope you'll talk to me and we can straighten this out.

I Love You,
Brian

Anna sank back into the hot water, letting the note slip through her fingers to the floor. She was so confused. Marcie had been her friend, yet she wanted to believe Brian. She just wasn't sure who to believe. *Would Brian really sleep with her friend?* The image of Marcie's car parked beside Brian's at the fire station flashed across her mind. Finally, she gave up. She found it much easier to drift back into the non-thinking stupor she had been in all day. She cleared her mind and let the hot water ease the tension in her muscles.

Her mental stupor continued the rest of the week, she refused to even look toward Brian's house as she came and went.

Nathan asked her every day when Brian was coming over. He clomped around the house in his cowboy boots and fire chief hat, anxiously waiting to show off his boots.

"Just like Brian's," he kept repeating. It hurt to hear his name said out loud and it hurt her that he had hurt her son. She wished she could give Brian and Marcie a lie detector test. She had trusted them both, how could she choose who to believe? It was easier to clear her mind of everything and keep making up excuses to Nathan.

She continued with their plan to take Magic on his visit to the retirement home. At least it was something she shared with Nathan and didn't remind her so much of Brian.

Everywhere she moved in her small trailer, there was some reminder of Brian. A lottery ticket held on her refrigerator by a magnet, his cowboy hat hanging from a hook by the door, he even had a shaving kit left in her bathroom and the smell of his cologne drove her to tears. She was doing her best to bring back the numbness she'd lived under for a year, but try as she might, she couldn't stop his beautiful face from appearing in her mind. Had Marcie been right? Was he a player and he'd only been playing with her feelings? She really couldn't make herself believe that.

Saturday, Anna put the blue vest on Magic and they set out. She had called ahead and set it up with the director of the rest home. He was happy to have them.

They arrived in the afternoon and met the director.

"My name is Walt." He took Anna's hand as she introduced herself, then Nathan's. He leaned down and patted Magic, talking to him as he rubbed his head. Magic enjoyed the attention and his tail thumped the floor.

Walt led them past a reception desk and through the lobby to a set of glass doors in the rear. The doors opened up onto a covered patio with metal tables and chairs. There was a huge grassy lawn sloping down to a small pond with a fountain spraying in the middle.

There were elderly people sitting at the tables, in wheelchairs on the lawn and some were strolling slowly across the grass. Magic took the lead, tugging on the leash until Anna followed him over to a lady in a wheelchair. She was slowly rocking back and forth in the chair as she stared at the pond. Magic walked slowly over to the wheelchair, placed his head in the lady's lap and stared up at her with his big, sad eyes, tail wagging constantly. She stopped rocking, looking at Magic with his head in her lap. Then the lady slowly raised her hand and placed it on Magic's head. She rubbed his head slowly and as she looked up at Anna and the director, Anna saw a smile light up one side of her face. The left side of her face seemed frozen, but Anna saw her eyes sparkle as she rubbed Magic's head.

Other people were making their way over to Magic now. He had become the center of attention as people gathered around, petting him and talking to him. Some of them began reminiscing with each other about dogs they had owned in the past.

After everyone had a chance to pet Magic, the director asked them to take a seat; Nathan took Magic's leash and had him perform tricks on the grassy lawn. The residents laughed and clapped with each trick, except for the lady Magic had first approached.

Anna learned from the director her name was Greta and she had had a stroke the previous year. She didn't laugh or clap her hands, but Anna could still see her eyes sparkle as she watched Magic.

After his show, Nathan led Magic back through the crowd, stopping as each person leaned down to pet Magic and talk to him. Magic pulled on the leash until Nathan followed him back to Greta, the lady in the wheelchair.

Anna saw her eyes light up again as Magic put his head in her lap. She leaned over and pulled Magic closer, hugging him to her for several minutes. When she let go and sat up, Anna could see one stray tear roll slowly down her cheek.

"Your dog is magic," Walt whispered to Anna.

"I know," Anna sniffed. Her eyes were misty too as Nathan rejoined them.

Afterward, Walt led them back to his office for a soda.

"Have a seat," he gestured to the two chairs in front of his desk as he pulled a soda from a small fridge for Nathan.

"Your show was amazing," he told Nathan with a happy smile. Nathan perked up.

"Magic loves doing tricks," he said. "We practice them almost every day."

"Well, it shows." Walt smiled at him. "I want you two to know, you are welcome back anytime. Our resident's certainly seemed to enjoy your visit."

"Can we come back next weekend, please mom?"

"Sure, sweetie. It's Magic's job now. To make people happy."

Anna stood and shook Walt's hand again as they made their way out.

She thought about their visit as she drove home. It was truly the only bright spot in her life lately. Nathan was bouncing on his seat, he was still so excited and proud of Magic. Anna reached over and tousled his head, then scratched Magic's neck.

That's the job I want, she thought. Making people happy. She had enjoyed herself more than she thought she would and seeing the sparkle in Greta's eyes had made her day.

"I wish Brian could've seen Magic's show," Nathan interrupted her thoughts. "We couldn't have done it without his training."

"I know, sweetie, I do too," she sighed wistfully, pain gripping her heart when she heard his name.

Chapter 12

Anna had Nathan and Magic to keep her mind off of Brian. She was still so hurt and confused with Brian and Marcie. Her instincts told her Brian wouldn't sleep with her friend, but Marcie had sounded so sincere. She only felt more confused when she thought about it; it was easier to numb her mind and her heart to the pain.

When she got home from work Wednesday evening, there was another small white envelope stuck in her door. I can't do this, she thought as she tossed it on the table with her mail and keys.

She kept glancing at it as she started dinner. *What the hell*, she finally grabbed it and angrily ripped it open. May as well get it over with. Anna was surprised when she pulled out a slip of paper instead of the letter she was expecting. *Another lottery ticket, really Brian?* She smiled in spite of herself as she hung it on the fridge.

She hadn't wanted to read some sappy letter apologizing for sleeping with her friend, but the lottery ticket made her think of Brian in a way she hadn't allowed herself.

She could see his face as she stood there, the way his slow grin lit up his deep blue eyes. She shook her head as she forced his face from her mind.

Brian, she thought as she heard a knock at the door. Her hand trembled as she opened the door, but it was Brenda on her step.

"Can I come in?" Brenda asked.

She took a step back to let Brenda enter, and then headed for the kitchen.

"Can I get you something, Brenda? I have fresh coffee."

"Sounds good," Brenda sat down at her table as Anna poured coffee for them both.

"You know Brian better than this, Anna," Brenda had barely waited for her to get seated.

"He wouldn't do this to you. I know Brian and he's too crazy about you to even look at Marcie. Hell, he hasn't looked at anyone else since he saw you in the grocery store. He would have asked you out before, but he knew you had turned down every offer you've had."

"But why would Marcie lie to me?"

"I don't know," Brenda shook her head as she thought about it. "I think she's jealous. I know Brian took her out on one date last year. He told Jason she just wasn't his type. But Marcie's been calling him off and on since then, trying to get him to go out again. Brian didn't want to hurt her feelings; he usually just made excuses."

"Maybe I should go and talk to her. She's very angry at me; she thinks I got her fired."

"The way I hear it, Mr. Jones caught her shoplifting."

Anna nodded. She was still confused. She thought she knew Marcie pretty well, but she also wouldn't of suspected her of stealing.

"Just think about it," Brenda said. "You know Brian better than anyone, do you really think he would sleep with your friend?"

She did think about it as she tossed and turned all night. She could still smell Brian's cologne on her pillow. She missed him so much, it made her feel sick. She tried everything to keep her mind off him, but every time she closed her eyes, she saw his beautiful face.

Sometime during the night, she heard Nathan cry out. As she sat up in bed, he was already at her door.

"I had a bad dream, can I get in your bed?"

"Come on Sweetie," Anna slid over to make room. Magic followed Nathan into her bed and slid in between them. Anna held them both as she drifted back to sleep.

She woke up a few hours later in the same position to the sound of a soft snore. She opened her eyes to see a black dog upside down beside her, his head on her pillow, paws in the air, snoring softly. She smiled as she held the two of them.

Anna remembered her lottery ticket as she rushed out the door the following morning. She hadn't slept very well, Brian's face appearing before her every time she closed her eyes. Now she had dark circles under her eyes and her face was pale, but she grabbed the ticket as she passed the refrigerator.

She remembered it again after she got to work, she pulled it from her pocket and ran it through the machine.

Nice, she thought with a grim smile, another loser.

She made it through the day, even though she felt almost too tired to stand.

Mr. Jones asked her to train Carrie, the

girl he'd hired to replace Marcie, and the
extra strain was definitely taking its toll.
Carrie chattered happily as Anna showed her
how to operate the scanner and cash register.
Carrie was young and blond and petite and
so bouncy with nervous excitement, it had
Anna's nerves rattled by the end of the day.
Patience, she kept reminding herself. It's not
Carrie's fault you were screwed over by the
only two people you've gotten close to in
this one horse town in the middle of
nowhere.

 She knew it wasn't really how she felt. She
was just exhausted and heartbroken. She
actually really loved the small town charm
and friendly people. It was so different from
the hustle and bustle of the city. She smiled
grimly and shook her head to clear it as
Carrie made a high-pitched squeak at the
register. Anna looked over Carrie's shoulder
 at the register, then smiled at the customer,
who looked like she was going to faint.

Carrie had hit the wrong key and the register
was reading One thousand four hundred and
sixty three dollars instead of one hundred

forty-six dollars and thirty cents.

"It's O.K. Mrs. Owens, we can fix it," she told her customer as she quickly voided the amount and had Carrie start over.

When she got home from work, Anna jumped in the shower before dinner. She felt so exhausted and worn down. She hadn't been eating well or sleeping much and her thoughts were constantly slipping back to Brian, no matter how hard she tried to make it stop. She'd thought she could return to the state of numbness she'd been in before meeting Brian, but unfortunately, her heart had a different plan. She knew without a doubt that even though he'd hurt her so badly, she was completely, totally and, regretfully in love with Brian.

Nathan was playing in the sandbox with the fire truck Brian had given him, Magic looking on happily and she thought a shower might wake her enough to spend some time with them. As she stepped from the shower, she heard Magic barking furiously.

Chapter 13

Brian decided to go fishing when he got home. Anything is better than pacing back and forth in that trailer, he thought, as he grabbed his fishing pole and headed out the door.

He walked toward the river behind the trailer park, wondering if his decision to give Anna some space had been the right one. He'd thought she would come to her senses in a day or two. He had to force himself not to pound on her door every day. He had finally gone by Marcie's apartment to confront her, but her roommate told him she had moved to Denver. He was wondering if he should start pounding on Anna's door every day until she agreed to talk to him. Brian was lost in his thoughts as he wandered through the trailer park and along the river bank. He didn't see the small boy climb over the fence and follow him. He walked several hundred yards down the river bank before settling into his favorite fishing spot and popping the tab on a beer.

He was thinking of the time he had brought Anna and Nathan to this spot when he heard a noise behind him. He spun around to see Nathan coming toward him. Nathan didn't slow down as he ran and jumped onto Brian's lap and hugged him tight.

Anna raced to the door in her towel and threw it open to see Magic jumping at the gate and barking. Not seeing Nathan anywhere in the small yard, she turned and ran back down the narrow hall to her room. Throwing on jeans and a shirt Brian had left there, she ran back through the trailer, stuffing her feet into sneakers as she went.

Magic was still jumping at the gate and barking as she got to him. She opened the gate and Magic bounded through it before she could stop him.

He raced toward the river with Anna trying to keep up. When he reached the tall grass along the riverbank, he slowed and ran back and forth, nose to the ground.

Anna caught up to him, calling Nathan's name repeatedly. She had never been so frightened in her life.

What if her little boy had fallen in the river? Her hands were shaking as she cupped them around her mouth and yelled Nathan's name as loud as she could.

Magic started trotting upriver, nose still to the ground and Anna followed along, hoping beyond hope that his nose would lead them to Nathan.

She jogged behind Magic through the tall grass and weeds for what seemed a long time, her heart racing, until she saw Magic take off at a run into a clearing on the river bank, straight into the arms of Brian and Nathan.

Brian stood up as Anna rushed up to

him, still holding Nathan in his arms.

Nathan had his arm around Brian's neck and wasn't letting go.

Anna saw her son clinging to Brian and felt a pain through her heart. She met Brian's eyes for a second, but that felt painful too.

Finally, seeing that her son wasn't going to release his grip around Brian's neck, she reached down and picked up the fishing pole and tackle box from the ground, turned without a word and started walking back.

When they got back to their own yard, Anna sat down on the trailer steps and hugged her son to her.

"Please don't ever do that to me again. You're gonna give mommy a heart attack." Brian watched as she held him for a minute, and then pulled Magic to her. She held the dog to her in a tight hug. "Thank you Magic," she said into his fur. She looked up at Brian as Magic and Nathan returned to their sandbox. Nathan seemed satisfied now that Brian had come back with them.

"You want to come in?" She already

knew the answer as she looked in his eyes.

He followed her inside and she started coffee, and then sat down at the table with him.

"What did Magic do?" he asked curiously.

"When I stepped out of the shower, I heard Magic barking. I threw on some clothes, ran outside and saw Nathan was missing. I think I nearly did have a heart attack. As soon as I opened the gate, Magic flew through it and started for the river, so I followed him. Once he was in the tall grass by the riverbank he put his nose to the ground and ran back and forth. I guess he picked up Nathan's scent because he turned and ran upriver straight to you. I wouldn't have known which way to go to start looking for him."

"That's pretty awesome." Brian looked into her eyes. "Have you had a chance to take him anywhere as a therapy dog yet?"

"Yeah, he was amazing. We took him to the retirement home and he seemed to love it. There was a lady in a wheelchair who had had a stroke. Magic made straight for her and I think he made a connection with her. He seemed to sense that she needed him more than anyone there."

"Wow, he's living up to his name, isn't he?

"Yeah, even more now that he led me straight to Nathan." Anna felt her pulse slowly returning to normal and her hands had stopped trembling.

"So," Brian changed the subject. "About us?"

Anna wanted to run away, but he had her locked into his mesmerizing stare. She had missed him more than she could say and seeing him with Nathan in his arms seemed like the most natural thing in the world to her. Brian reached across the table and took her hand in his. She felt the familiar tingle at his touch. He still hadn't taken his eyes from hers.

"You know I wouldn't sleep with Marcie, don't you? Or anyone else for that matter?"

Anna stared into his eyes. It was all right there for her to see. She felt like she could drown in his steel-blue eyes, she could see only trust and honesty in them.

Why did I ever doubt him in the first place? She reached over the table and kissed him longingly. He stood up and pulled her up into a bear hug.

"I believe you," she whispered into his neck, a single tear squeezing from her eye and rolling down her cheek. When Brian sat her back on her feet, she turned around to find Nathan behind them.

"Come here, Chief." Brian reached down and scooping Nathan into his powerful arms, swung him around the trailer until he squealed in delight. Magic barked and ran with them as they played until Anna shooed them all out the door, telling them to take it outside while she started dinner. She tried to make her voice sound stern, but she couldn't keep the laughter from her tone. It was just so wonderful to hear the noise and laughter again. Her heart felt light and full as she started dinner. She felt foolish to have avoided talking to Brian for so long. And it had really only taken a look into those beautiful eyes to see the truth.

They made love slowly that night and Brian held her tight as she drifted off to sleep. Anna's heart felt whole again as she cuddled in his arms.

Nathan was back to himself again with Brian back in his life. He had moped about the house for weeks, asking Anna every day when Brian was coming by.

Now, Brian wrestled on the floor with him and helped him bathe Magic, he even showed up one evening after work with a new fishing pole for him.

Anna felt tears sting her eyes as she watched the two of them together. Her son was obviously as crazy about Brian as she was. She had never known such happiness came from the smallest, most simple things in life. A simple picnic, a leisurely horseback ride and even the time spent training Magic were suddenly the best things in life.

Anna continued her research whenever she had time to stop at the library. She learned everything she could about service dogs and therapy animals. She knew it was something she wanted to do with her life. *But how do I go about it? I would never have the kind of money I need to get started.* She thought about it as she lay awake at night, listening to Brian's soft snore beside her. She called the director of the local hospital and after being placed on hold and switched over to numerous people, she finally got a Mr. Stevens on the line. She explained what she wanted to do and he set up a time for a visit.

Anna left Nathan with Brian while she took Magic to the hospital after work. She didn't know what sort of patients they would be seeing and she didn't want to expose Nathan to anything that would be traumatic. Magic was beginning to understand his blue vest meant time to go to work and be on his best behavior. He trotted proudly through the door of the hospital, getting stares and pats on the head as he went.

The receptionist phoned Mr. Stevens and he met them in the lobby.

He led Anna to the third floor and left them in the hands of the head nurse on duty, Nurse Davies. She took Anna's hand warmly as she led them toward a patient's room.

"Mr. Stevens informed me you would be stopping by. I've heard of this kind of thing in the cities, but I never expected it in this small town. I have just the patient for you. No one here has been able to reach her. We have a therapist that sees her every day, but nothing's helped. She doesn't speak and barely eats. It's as if she's given up on life."

Anna nodded as they walked. Nurse Davies wasn't exactly giving her a chance to speak as she chattered on. "Her name is Lisa. I'll stay by the door to make sure she's o.k."

Anna felt a little nervous as they reached the door. Nurse Davies knocked once, and then pushed the door open. Anna saw a young woman on the bed, staring straight ahead, her face swollen with the remains of bruising on both cheekbones and a black eye that was mostly healed.

She led Magic slowly to the bed; he put his front paws on it as Lisa's head swiveled slowly to look at him. She appeared to be in her mid- twenties, but it was kind of hard to tell with the shape her face was in. She reached a hand out tentatively to Magic. It was all the invitation he needed. Before Anna could stop him, he leaped and plopped himself on the bed beside Lisa, licking her hand. Anna glanced around at Ms. Davies. She smiled from her place by the door and winked at Anna. Magic lay down on the bed beside Lisa and she put her arm around him. He rolled onto his back for a tummy rub. Anna dropped the leash and took a step back. No one had spoken a word, but she felt as if anything she said would break the magic spell that was unfolding.

No one noticed as Nurse Davies quietly closed the door and went back to her station. She'd seen all she needed to see.

Anna walked around the bed and stared

out the window. She wanted to give the girl some time with Magic.

She looked around when she heard Lisa crying softly. Lisa had both arms wrapped around Magic and was crying into his fur. Magic wagged his tail and licked her face as if to say, 'I'll make it all better for you.'

She cried for a while as Anna looked out the window, wondering what had happened to this girl to bring her to such a state. Whatever happened to her, she's an emotional mess, she thought with a wry smile. *Hell, I oughtta know.*

When Lisa had cried herself out, Anna turned to check on her. Magic was still lying alongside her as she stroked his silky coat.

Anna finally spoke as she turned back to the window, but she didn't speak directly to Lisa. Instead, she just started talking. She talked about the ranch and Tango and Ladybug, keeping her back to Lisa and never saying anything that required an answer. She talked about the picnics and the peace and beauty of the stream and countryside. She told how quiet it was out on the ranch, no sound except for birds chirping, the creak of saddle leather and the breeze moving through the grasses out on the plains. She told of Tango's wild run around the barrels and how, although scary, it was so exhilarating she couldn't wait to do it again. She described the fireworks show, lying on her back underneath the show and how it looked as if the stars were falling down from heaven. After she had talked for an hour with Lisa holding Magic tight and stroking his fur the entire time, Nurse Davies came back for her.

"It's almost time for dinner," she said.

Anna took it as her cue to leave, she went around the bed and picked up Magic's leash. As she let go of Magic, Lisa made eye contact with Anna.

"Please come back again," she whispered. Her voice was a hoarse croak, as if it was rusty from lack of use.

"I would love too," Anna smiled at her as she led Magic away.

Ms. Davies led her back to the nurse's

station. "Did I just hear her speak to you?" she asked.

"Yes, you did," Anna said proudly.

"Her husband beat her, you know. He almost beat her to death this time. He's in jail for assault."

"This time?"

"Yeah, it's not the first time, but we must make sure it's the last. I'm pretty sure he meant to kill her. It's been going on for several years, but she would never press charges against him."

"Why not?" Anna was shocked.

"Because she knew he would kill her," Nurse Davies said angrily.

"Can I come back again this week?"

"Yeah, same time?"

Anna nodded, lost in thought.

She drove home slowly thinking of the physical and emotional abuse Lisa had endured. She couldn't imagine living in that kind of fear.

She told Brian about Lisa as they lay in Bed that night, her head on his shoulder.

"I know it's what I want to do with my life," she told him. "I would love to have a ranch like your parent's have, but with therapy horses and dogs, maybe I could raise service dogs for people too. If I can help even one person the way Magic has helped Nathan, it would make me so happy."

Brian hugged her tight. "I'm sure you'll make it happen some way."

Chapter 14

Brian invited them to the ranch the following night to watch a Meteor show. "They are forecasting around fifty meteors per hour," he told them. "It gets really dark out on the ranch. We should have a great view."

"Sounds great," Anna told him, "But you have to let me take Magic by the hospital first."

Anna got a call during dinner from a Mrs. Phelps. She was the therapist who had been treating Lisa.

"I heard about your visit yesterday," she began, and I want you to know, whatever you're doing, keep it up."

She told Anna, Lisa had finally talked to her a little bit. "Mostly about you and Magic, but it's a start."

Anna thanked her and hung up, a big smile on her face. She felt such a warm feeling wash over her, knowing that in some small way, she and Magic had made a difference in this girl's life.

Anna's second visit to the hospital went even better. Magic jumped on the bed with Lisa while Anna stood at the window and talked.

Lisa had a little more life to her eyes today and a little more color in her cheeks.

Anna talked about her life in Denver and how much it had changed, how stressful it had been fighting rush hour traffic day after day for a career that didn't make her happy. She talked about her dream of someday owning a ranch that could be used for helping people.

After she had talked on for a bit, she turned to find Lisa and Magic both looking at her, Magic held tight in Lisa's arms as she listened.

"Go on," Lisa said. "Tell me more about the horses."

Anna talked on and on, eventually sitting on the side of the bed, her back still to Lisa. Magic had rolled onto his back, all four paws sticking in the air as Lisa gently rubbed his stomach.

When Nurse Davies came to get her, Anna turned to face Lisa.

"There's supposed to be an awesome meteor shower tonight, maybe you can see it from your window."

Lisa smiled at her. "Thank you, I'll watch for it," she said softly.

Anna heard her name as she and Magic reached the door. When she looked back, Lisa smiled at her. "Can you come back again?" Her voice was small and weak, but Anna heard her.

"We're looking forward to it, aren't we Magic?" She reached down and patted his shoulder as she spoke. Magic's tail wagged in agreement.

Anna raced back to pick up Brian and

Nathan. They had packed a picnic while they waited. They jumped into her truck and headed out to the ranch. Brian directed her across the ranch to a flat spot on top of a grassy hill.

She parked beside an old windmill with a water tank beside it. The windmill creaked as it turned slowly in the breeze.

Magic ran and sniffed through the grass while they had their picnic on the back of her truck.

It was beginning to get dark as they finished eating and cleaned up.

They all lay back onto the bed of the pickup as the darkness closed in, watching one star after another getting brighter in the sky, the only sound an occasional creak of the old windmill.

As full darkness surrounded them, Anna was surprised. She had never seen such darkness in Denver. There was no light as far as the eye could see. Except for the stars, she thought peacefully. Millions of stars, more stars than she had ever seen in her life.

"Oh!" Nathan gasped as the first meteor shot across the sky. Then another and another.

Brian took her hand as they lay side by side in her rusty old truck, listening to Nathan's excitement as he saw more and more meteors.

"I don't think life gets any better than this," she turned her head to look at Brian.

"No, it doesn't." He squeezed her hand as more meteors shot across the sky, so bright they hurt her eyes in the blackness, before they burned out and disappeared.

Anna had to work the following weekend, but she still stopped by the hospital after work.

Lisa was sitting up in bed now, the swelling was gone from her face and she had a sparkle in her eyes as Magic bounded through the door. She was holding conversations with Anna now; she mostly wanted to know about the ranch and horses and dogs.

"I've always loved animals," she said,

hugging Magic to her, "but I was never allowed to have any."

"I'm sure you'll have your chance. You can do anything you want with your life, be whatever you want to be."

"Thank you, Anna. I hope I'm strong enough." They grew quiet as Lisa scratched Magic behind the ear. Anna remembered thinking the same thing about herself this past year.

"I'm sure you are," she said quietly.

She went back to the window to give Lisa time with Magic. She could hear Lisa talking to him as she rubbed his head.

As Anna stood looking out the window, Lisa began talking to her. Her voice was weak and shaky at first, but it grew stronger as she talked.

"Things were good between Joe and I when we were first married," she began slowly. "Joe lost his job a couple years ago when the recession hit and he changed." Lisa paused, pain evident in her voice, and then continued.

"I found a job as a waitress and when I came home every day, he would be drunk. He hated the fact that I was supporting him. I told him over and over it wasn't true, we had his unemployment checks, too. He only got angrier each time it came up, until one day he slapped me. He apologized later and swore it would never happen again, but it did. It got worse as time went on; I tried to leave but he threatened me. He would apologize later and cry in my arms. He said he couldn't live without me."

Lisa took a deep, unsteady breath, and then continued.

"Last week one of the waitresses was out sick; I worked a double shift every day. Then one day, the restaurant was really busy and I got home late. Joe was drunker than usual and angrier than usual. He said I was worthless because the house was a mess and I hadn't come home and cooked his dinner. I had been on my feet for eleven hours and I think I snapped at him. He started hitting me and he wouldn't stop. He knocked me to the floor and kept punching me and kicking me until I passed out." Anna turned to see tears rolling slowly down Lisa's cheeks.

"I was here when I woke up and nurse Davies told me Joe is in jail. I'm scared for my life, Anna and I don't know what I'm going to do when I leave here. I can't go home or back to my job. I just want to disappear," she sounded so sad and dejected, Anna turned from the window and took Lisa in her arms. She held the girl as she cried, Magic between them on the bed, his head on Lisa's lap.

When she returned home, Brian had already started dinner. He turned from the stove and kissed her when she entered. She told him how well her visit had gone and how much she was enjoying it, then she wrapped her arms around him and held on for a bit, thinking how lucky she was to have found such a wonderful man.

As they were sitting down to dinner, Anna's cell phone rang. She was shocked to hear Marcie's voice. She looked at Brian and mouthed the word 'Marcie' as she moved toward the bedroom.

"I called to apologize," Marcie began. "I know you didn't get me fired. When I went back for my last paycheck, Mr. Jones showed me his videos. And I didn't sleep with Brian. I only said that to hurt you and I'm sorry." Anna heard a sniffle, it sounded like Marcie was crying. "I guess I was a little jealous, too. I kind of felt like he rejected me, then went after you."

Did he? She wasn't sure, but she knew Marcie could never have been Brian's type. She really couldn't imagine the two of them together.

"It's o.k. Marcie. I'm glad you told me the truth. I forgive you."

"Thank you, Anna. I've missed you. I'm living in Denver now and I got a job at a nightclub."

"I'm glad for you, Marcie. That's sounds perfect for you." No way was she going to tell Marcie she had missed her too. Honestly, she hadn't given her another thought. But she wasn't planning on giving her another chance to cause trouble. Marcie had already caused everyone enough pain. They hung up on a friendly note and Anna returned to dinner.

As they lay in bed that night, her head on his shoulder after making love, she told Brian what Marcie had said.

"I hope she stays in Denver and out of both our lives," he said angrily. "I always knew that girl was trouble, that's why I wouldn't go out with her again."

They were silent for a bit as Anna worked up her nerve. Then finally she told him what was on her mind.

"It's pointless to keep paying rent for a trailer that is only storing your boxes," she said lightly. "And you're here most of the time anyway."

"I thought you'd never ask!" He didn't wait for her to finish as he took her in his arms and kissed her fervently.

Brian finally got his boxes unpacked over the next couple of weeks and settled in. It felt so natural to Anna and Nathan, it seemed like Brian had always been there with them. They seemed like any happy, well-adjusted family to anyone who saw them.

Brian continued his weekly lottery ticket purchase. Every Wednesday Anna saw him put a new one on the refrigerator. It always made her smile, and she occasionally chided him for wasting his money, but she secretly loved it.

One week, when she checked the ticket at the store, they had actually won four dollars.

"We won," she laughed with Brian as she waved the four dollars at him.

"See, I told you," he kissed her as he laughed, "and you told me the odds were so bad, we'd never win!"

Chapter15

The summer had been a whirlwind for Anna, but now it was winding down as she began getting Nathan ready for school.

She still made her trips by the hospital and she and Nathan visited the retirement home a few more times.

Magic still went straight to the lady in the wheelchair when they visited. He always seemed to brighten her day.

They began seeing other patients in the hospital and Anna took Nathan with her to the children's ward. The children played with Magic and laughed as Nathan had him do a few of his tricks.

But for Anna, her visits with Lisa were the most special. She had become very fond of the girl and she was proud of the fact that she and Magic had helped to bring some joy back into a life that had been filled with pain.

She was shocked when she stopped by Lisa's room one evening to find it empty. The room was clean, crisp and white as if it had never been occupied by a forlorn young girl. Anna ran back to the nurse's station to find Nurse Davies.

"She's healed and gone, but I'm not allowed to tell you where she was taken."
Anna frowned as she studied Ms. Davies face. She was hurt that Lisa hadn't wanted to stay in touch with her when she left the hospital. She felt they had formed a bond over the weeks.

"I can tell you, she didn't go to her house." Nurse Davies said kindly. "I wish I could say more, but it's important in these kinds of cases for her husband to never find her. If he ever gets out of jail. With the internal injuries Lisa had, it's possible he could be charged with attempted murder. If a neighbor hadn't heard her screams and pulled him off, I'm sure he would have killed her."

Anna shuddered as she thought about what Lisa had gone through. She hoped wherever she was, she would find a way to heal emotionally and find happiness.

"Thank you, Ms. Davies. Nathan and I will be back next week to visit the kids if it's o.k."

"We are happy to have you here. I think our entire staff has grown attached to Magic."

Anna nodded thoughtfully as she led Magic toward the elevators, her mind still on Lisa. She hadn't realized how painful it would be to part with the people whose lives they had touched.

They went riding again the following weekend. It was to be a family outing again with a longer ride around the ranch. But, it was also a working ride this time, he explained. They had miles of fence to ride and pregnant cows to bring in closer to the barns before winter set in.

As they set off Saturday morning in Brian's jeep, Anna was surprised when he passed the entrance to the ranch, then turned off the main road and headed west on a smaller two lane blacktop.

"If you're kidnapping us, no one's going to pay a cent!" Anna joked.

"I want to show you something," Brian said mysteriously.

Anna surveyed the landscape as he drove through the Animas valley. The river wound its way through a wide valley with rolling hills rising on each side. The grass in the valley was a richer green than the prairie grasses across the hills.

"It's beautiful here," she said wistfully.

Brian turned in beneath a steel arch onto a dirt drive that wound through the valley to a two story white farmhouse with a covered porch and white railings wrapping around it. She could see an enormous red barn set off to the right. The paint was faded and weathered, but to Anna it was beautiful. Beside the barn was a large corral with several ranch horses milling about.

As Brian stopped in front of the house, a skinny elderly lady with white curly hair stepped out onto the porch. She shaded her eyes from the sun's glare as she greeted them.

"Good morning," Brian called as they all climbed out of his jeep, Magic bounding ahead.

"Are you the young man on the phone?"

"Yes, ma'am," Brian tipped his cowboy hat to her. "I'm Brian, this is Anna and Nathan and that's Magic," he said, pointing at Magic running through the grass, nose to the ground.

"Well, come on in. Nice to see young folks around here again. It's been a while. My name is Shirley White." Anna followed her inside, still trying to figure out what they were doing there.

"Can I get you folks something, I just made iced tea?"

"Sure," Anna said as Nathan nodded shyly. She didn't really want any tea, but she didn't want to be rude.

They sat around a large kitchen table as Shirley poured iced tea for them, and then dropped into a chair at one end of the table. She had a stack of ledgers on the table in front of her, she picked them up and passed them to Brian.

"All the recent cattle tallies are there," she told him. Anna still had no idea what was going on.

"If I get ten percent down, I can carry the note." Shirley told Brian.

Anna's mouth dropped open as she stared at Brian. This was language she understood from her days as a realtor.

"You want to buy this place?" she asked him, astonished.

"I would love to," he answered longingly.

"Why don't I show you and Nathan around while Brian goes over the books," Shirley told Anna.

She led them through a big living room

with an enormous rock fireplace at one end, a large picture window along the front looking out over a breathtaking view of the valley. From the foyer, she took them up a flight of stairs through four large bedrooms.

"The views from here are amazing," Anna was awestruck, looking across the valley toward the river. She could see another herd of ranch horses grazing alongside the river.

The cottonwoods were brilliant with fall colors, bright yellow, with green and softer hues of yellow mingling together.

"The valley and river are part of this ranch." Shirley told her. "Water rights are one of the most important things out here."

"It's so beautiful, it looks like a postcard." Anna was amazed at the peaceful beauty stretching out before her. The big house was obviously old and worn, but after a year in a small trailer, Anna found it beautiful.

"Is that a bunkhouse?" Anna pointed to a small white cottage with peeling paint, situated just past the barn.

"Used to be," Shirley said. "Now it's a guesthouse. Although it's mostly just sat empty the last few years."

After they had wandered through each room, Shirley led them back downstairs and out to the barn. Anna couldn't believe the size of it as they entered. The big red barn made the farmhouse look small by comparison. The barn had a huge opening at each end with stalls lining each side. A tack room was off to the right as they entered. Saddles lined the walls, bridles and tack hanging from hooks over them. Nathan ran through the barn with Magic, looking in stall after stall. Most stood empty except for one at the far end. As they reached it, they heard the bray of a donkey. A grey face with long ears appeared over the stall door.

"That's Jenny," Shirley told him as she and Anna caught up to him. "She's only inside today to get her hooves trimmed.

Nathan giggled as the donkey nuzzled his ear and blew air onto his neck.

Anna turned as she heard Brian coming through the barn. He was looking around as he walked slowly over to them.

"I'm sure you can see from the books this place turns a decent profit," Shirley said as he reached them. "I would never part with it if I weren't getting too old to keep it up. Both my son's bought adjoining ranches in the Texas panhandle. They've been begging me for years to move out there and help with the grandchildren."

Brian put his arm across Anna's shoulder as they wandered out to the corral.

The ranch horses were curious and came over to sniff them. Anna scratched their faces as they put their heads over the bars.

"I'll leave you folks alone unless you have any other questions," Shirley said.

"We'll be in touch," Brian shook her hand.
"Thank you for the tour," Anna shook hands with her, too. "Your place is beautiful."

"What was that all about?" She asked as they climbed back into the jeep. "Are you seriously thinking of buying this place?"

"I don't know, Anna." Brian sighed. "It's a lot of money, but it is a working cattle ranch. Everything goes with it. The cattle, horses, everything. It would be awesome if we could come up with the down payment. And, you would have your place to start your therapy ranch."

Anna grew quiet as she thought about it. Living in that huge old farmhouse after her small, cramped trailer. Horses and cattle and beautiful views everywhere she looked. She looked around longingly as Brian headed back down the drive, then she shook her head quickly, trying to erase the thought from her mind. She was determined not to get caught up in that world again. She was perfectly happy with what she had now.

Chapter 16

Brian's family laughed and joked with each other as they rode, their horses trotting along, keeping pace with each other.

They rode south for a while before coming on a herd of fat black cattle. They rode in a wide circle around them, and then slowly started pushing them back toward the corrals. Ben really only wanted the pregnant cows, steers and bulls he cut out as they rode. Anna had never seen a cutting horse in action before. It was a beautiful thing to watch. Ben seemed to sit still on the horse, his reins hanging loose as his horse dodged back and forth, pushing each cow where he wanted it. When there were only the pregnant cows left, they used their horses to keep them bunched tightly together, slowly pushing them north.

As she rode, Anna's thoughts kept returning to the ranch they had seen. She knew there was no way she could afford it. Her salary barely kept the bills paid. A savings account was out of the question. She had to keep reminding herself that it didn't matter. Nathan and Brian and Magic and the peacefulness and good times on this ranch were more than anyone could wish for.

Chapter 17

Anna asked Nurse Davies about other places she could take Magic for a visit. She and Nathan were enjoying it so much, but they couldn't overstay their welcome at the hospital. She gave Anna a number to a homeless shelter in town.

Anna called the director to see if it would be o.k. to bring Magic for a visit.

"We would love it." A Mrs. Jenks told her. "We don't get much of that kind of thing around here.

Nathan wanted to go fishing with Brian so Anna took Magic to the shelter alone. There was a small group of men and women gathered around a T.V. at one end of a large, open room. Anna approached slowly with Magic as people began to notice her and stare. Maybe this was a bad idea, she thought as the room grew silent. She wasn't feeling the good-natured welcome she was used to at the retirement home and hospital.

Magic took the lead as usual, pulling on his leash until she followed him past the uneasy stares over to a couch by the T.V. As people stepped to the side as if they were afraid of Magic, she could see a young girl on the couch. Anna caught her breath as Lisa looked up at her. Lisa's face lit up as Magic jumped on the couch beside her, rolling onto his back for his usual tummy rub. Anna dropped down on the couch and gave Lisa a warm hug.

"It's so good to see you. I've missed you," she croaked as she fought back the tears. "I never thought I'd see you again."

"I'm sorry, Anna, I'm not supposed to tell anyone where I am," Lisa was crying as she hugged Anna. "I wanted to contact you, but they won't let me make any calls. My husband is out on bail; he can't find me."

Her voice rose as she thought about what he would do to her if he found her.

"Don't worry, your secret is safe with me," Anna smiled at her as she dropped onto the couch beside her.

Other people wandered over when they saw Magic upside down on the couch with Lisa, his head hanging part of the way off the seat, tongue lolling as she rubbed his stomach. His tail thumped the couch as an older lady scratched his chin. Within moments, Magic was surrounded by a crowd, rubbing, patting and playing with him.

Anna stayed at the shelter until dinnertime, visiting with Lisa when she could. She promised her she would be back as soon as she could. Lisa kneeled on the floor and held Magic in her arms for a bit before she would let them go.

"Thank you," she said as she looked up at Anna.

Chapter 18

The clerks were excited when Anna got to work on Thursday.

"We sold a winning lottery ticket." Jeannie told her as Carrie jumped up and down with excitement.

Anna immediately felt her pockets. "I always forget the damn thing," she laughed.

"You should go get it on your break," Jeannie's voice trembled with excitement.

"I don't put a lot of stock in those things," Anna refused to let their excitement affect her. "I'll bring it tomorrow. Anyway, the winner will probably claim it today."

"Yeah, I guess you're right." Jeannie had lost some of her excitement.

Anna stayed busy the rest of the day and her mind roamed back to Lisa whenever she had a free minute.

She completely forgot the lottery excitement until she raced out the door Friday morning. She was already in her truck when Brian came out to her. She put the window down as he waved the ticket at her. He kissed her as he handed it to her.

"You're beautiful, you know," he said as he touched her face.

"You're a good liar and I'm gonna be late." She kissed him again, then backed her truck into the street, shoving the lottery ticket into her pocket as she went.

It was another busy day at the store. Anna had a line of customers when someone handed her a lottery ticket and asked her to check it for him. Anna took it from him and ran it through the machine.

"I sure could use twenty million dollars," the kid said as she ran it.

"Yeah, wouldn't that be nice," Anna was

reminded of her own ticket still in her pocket.

"You know we sold a winning ticket in this store and it hasn't been claimed?"

The kid's face fell as the machine only beeped once instead of the sing-song noise it made when a ticket is a winner.

"Sorry, better luck next time." She felt bad for him, but what could she do? She was well used to losing after all the tickets Brian had bought her.

She pulled her ticket out of her pocket and set it beside her register, but she still had a line of people waiting. She left it there while she took care of customers.

The store cleared out some by late afternoon and Jeannie came over to her as she ran her ticket, clasping her hands together under her chin in her excitement.

"I just know it's you. You're gonna be a millionaire."

"Yeah, or maybe Brian's gonna go broke buying these damn things," she laughed.

She slid the ticket through the machine and

heard the single beep of a losing ticket. Jeannie's arms dropped to her sides and she let her breath out in a whoosh as Anna shrugged her shoulders.

"Maybe next time," she consoled Jeannie.

Anna wasn't even disappointed. She hadn't had her hopes up like Jeannie.

The store was busy again and Anna was running her register when she looked up to see Brian in her line. She smiled at him, and then went back to the customer in front of her. She was helping an elderly gentleman put his bags in the grocery cart, and then she turned back to her register.

Brian was in front of her now and he had a line of people waiting behind him. She looked up and smiled at him as she began sliding his items across the scanner. She looked down when she didn't hear the telltale beep of the scanner. She had a small black box in her hand. That's odd, she thought. I don't remember anything like this in the store. She swiped it again. Still no beep. She saw Brian's gorgeous grin as she looked up at him, confusion wrinkling her brow.

"Open it," he said. Anna looked at the other people in line, they were all smiling at her too.

She opened the box as Brian came around to her side of the register.

"You can't…" she started, but her breath caught as she saw the sparkle of the diamond ring in the box. Brian was behind her register now and he dropped to one knee. Anna looked up to see other patrons of the store had stopped with their carts to watch. She looked at Jeannie and saw she had tears running down her face, her hands covering her mouth. The store had gone silent as everyone stood as if frozen, watching the spectacle play out before them.

"I got something to ask you, Anna," she turned her eyes back to Brian and the box in her hand. He took the box from her, removed the ring and held it on his index finger, shining up at her.

"Anna Marie James, would you do me the honor of marrying me and making me the happiest man in the world?"

"Yes," she whispered as Brian slipped the ring on her finger and stood up, picking her up with him into a bear hug. He stepped from behind the register with her and spun her around as he hugged her. The entire store erupted into applause and cheers. She looked around at the crowd that had gathered as she realized tears were spilling down her cheeks too.

Brian set her down as the crowd looked on, still smiles and cheers all around.

"I have a wedding gift for you," he said as he pulled a folded paper from his pocket. Anna wiped her eyes as she took the paper into her trembling hands.

"You know there's nothing I need but you and Nathan and Magic, don't you? There's nothing else you can give me that will ever compare?"

"Oh, give it back then." Brian grabbed at the paper in her hand playfully as she moved it out of his reach, spinning away from him as she unfolded it.

"Brian, you can't…how did you do this?" She was looking at a receipt for a down payment on Shirley's ranch.

"You know we can't afford this? How did you even come up with the down payment?"

"I had some in savings and I borrowed the rest from my parents."

"Brian, we can't!" Anna was aghast. "I won't do that to your family. It would take years to pay them back."

"It'll be o.k. Anna, trust me." She saw his slow grin spreading across his face and felt a little better. Hopefully he had some sort of plan.

"I can't believe this, Brian. The ranch is really ours?" She was moving back to her register and the customers still waiting in her line.

"It's really ours. Horses, cattle, the donkey, all of it. Now you can start your therapy ranch."

Anna was still in awe as she reached her

register. She couldn't believe this amazingly sweet, gentle man had done so much for her and Nathan.

"Oh, one more thing, Anna." She had been about to begin ringing up her next customer's items. Her line had grown incredibly long, although it was hard to tell which ones were in line and which ones had stopped to watch her and Brian. "Could you check this lottery ticket for me?"

"Sorry for the wait, sir," she told her customer as she took Brian's ticket.

"I'm in no hurry, young lady," he replied, "I've enjoyed the show."

Other customers were starting on their way as the excitement died down, pushing their carts toward the aisles, still talking about the romantic young man proposing in a grocery store.

Anna slid Brian's ticket through the machine and everyone in the store froze again as they heard the sing-song beeps of the computer. Anna's eyes widened as she looked at the readout.

"You won?" She squinted her eyes at the red numbers on the machine, still trying to understand what she was seeing. Her mind felt numb as she looked at it. She turned to look at Brian, his grin turning into an ever widening smile.

"Yep, twenty million dollars."

Anna looked around the store. Customers were cheering and laughing as they realized Brian was the big winner everyone had been talking about. Jeannie was openly crying and laughing at the same time as she jumped up and down and Carrie squealed and clapped as she bounced around. Brian picked her up again and spun her around as customers cheered and clapped.

"We won, baby." He sat her down amid the applause from the crowd.

"I can't believe it." Anna felt frozen from shock. This was like something from a dream. It couldn't really be happening, could it?

"I think you should go home, Anna." She turned to find Mr. Jones behind her.

"I'll run your register, you two go home and celebrate."

"Thank you, sir." Brian answered for her. Anna was still numb from the shock of it all and hadn't found her voice yet. Brian swept her into his arms and carried her out the door amid more raucous applause from the crowd.

Two months later

"That looks like the last of it." Brian dropped the last remaining box from the rental truck on the floor of their new home. Anna had been wandering from room to room, still trying to make herself believe she wasn't dreaming. She stopped in front of the huge windows looking over the valley and river.

It was a winter picture outside now, but she knew she could have everything in place by spring to start her therapy ranch. She just hadn't figured out yet what kind of therapy ranch she wanted or how to go about it. Brian put his arms around her and pulled her back into his chest. They stood that way for a while, basking in the happiness of their new home and ranch. She knew as she stood there she would never need to chase the

American Dream again, thanks to Magic and the magic of Brian.

"There's only one more thing I need to do," she told Brian as she leaned back into his broad chest. She explained her idea to him as they stood there looking over their valley and he squeezed her tight as he thought about what a lucky man he was to have found such a thoughtful, loving woman to share his life with.

Chapter 19

Anna dropped Nathan at school the following morning then drove through town to put her plan into action. She headed to the homeless shelter with Magic by her side. She'd been there countless times over the past two months to visit with Lisa and the other residents. Anna had grown so close to Lisa that she thought of her more as a sister than a friend. They had laughed together and played with Magic, but there was always an underlying current of sadness about Lisa that never seemed to fade. She had been through so much in her young life, Anna wondered if she would ever be able to put her complete trust in anyone again. Except for Magic.

Lisa was crazy about that dog. Anna felt sure he had helped Lisa almost as much he had Nathan.

Lisa was having breakfast when Anna arrived. She left the table to drop onto the floor and give Magic a hug. He wagged his tail and licked her neck as she pulled him close.

"Is there somewhere we can talk?" Anna whispered.

Lisa looked up at her from the floor, Magic still cuddled in her arms.

"My room," she croaked, her expression near panic as she glanced around the room.

Anna followed her down the hall with Magic by her side. When they entered the sparse room, Anna saw it was more of a dorm with several beds and dressers and nothing else to give it any life. They sat on Lisa's bed as Anna outlined her plan.

"I would like for you to come live at the ranch," she began. "There's a guest house that's yours if you want it. There is plenty of work on the ranch if you're willing, although I can't pay you a very big salary."

Lisa's eyes had grown wide as Anna talked

and now tears were forming, ready to spill down her cheeks. Magic sensed her mood and jumped on the bed and with his tail wagging, licked away her tears as they rolled down her cheeks.

"Are you serious?" Lisa looked at Anna over Magic's back as she pulled him close to her.

Anna stood up and hugged Lisa with Magic caught between them.

"Thank you, Anna," Lisa whispered in her forlorn way. "I don't know much about ranching, but I'll work my butt off to try and repay all the kindness you've shown me."

Lisa gathered her few belongings and they left together, Anna describing her ideas for a therapy ranch as she drove.

Once she had her settled into the guest house, Lisa followed Anna back to the big farmhouse to help with her unpacking

Brian was out on horseback, checking on his cows and riding the fences. They had the house to themselves as they ran from room to room, giggling like schoolgirls. Then they settled down to the work of unpacking as they started in the kitchen, emptying boxes of dishes. They shared an easy comaraderie as they worked; Anna felt like she'd known Lisa forever. She could see the tension easing from the girl's shoulders as they unpacked box after box, chatting amiably.

They took a break in the afternoon. Anna made coffee and they took their steaming mugs with them to the front porch. Shirley had left behind two white, wooden rockers and they dropped into them, looking across the stunning vista as they rocked. Brian came riding up just then and Anna was still stunned at how striking he looked in his cowboy hat and boots.

"Thought you girls were supposed to be unpacking," he playfully chided them as he stepped off the horse, leaving the reins trailing to the ground.

He stepped forward and shook Lisa's hand as Anna introduced them, then tipped his hat to her as Lisa giggled, overwhelmed by his charm.

"Just taking a break," Anna replied. "What about you? I thought you were out chasing cows around."

"A man's gotta eat." He swatted her playfully with his hat as he passed her and went inside.

The following afternoon, the girls were still working at the unpacking while Nathan played with Magic and the donkey, Jenny, in the yard.

When they heard a car coming up the drive, Anna left the bedroom, where they'd been putting away Nathan's things, to see who it was. Lisa huddled in Nathan's closet where she'd been working, a look of fear on her face, sure her husband had found her here.

"I'll see who it is, you stay here," Anna told her as she headed down the stairs.

She was surprised and delighted to see Mrs. Wilson step out of the passenger side of the car, but she didn't recognize the dark-haired young man behind the wheel. He looked almost afraid to open his door and step out, Anna noted as Mrs. Wilson reached her and gave her a warm hug.

"This is my grandson, Michael." Mrs. Wilson turned to see her grandson slowly stepping from the car, keeping a wary eye on Nathan playing in the yard with Jenny and Magic. The donkey was dropping her head to the ground and chasing Magic and Nathan at a trot around the yard. Then she would run at a gallop as they turned and chased her. The three of them were becoming fast friends.

Magic recognized Mrs. Wilson and came at a dead run straight to her feet, where he stopped, sat down and gazed up at her lovingly, black tail wagging. Mrs. Wilson stooped to pet Magic as Anna shook Michael's hand.

"It's nice to meet you, Michael."

"It's Mike," the dark-haired young man gruffly corrected her. He looked to be in his mid- twenties, Anna thought. A good-looking guy, but his eyes had a haunted, untrusting look about them as he kept glancing around the property, as if he expected a criminal to be lurking behind every bush, it seemed to Anna.

"Won't you both come in?" Anna asked. "I've got fresh coffee on, or I could make tea if you prefer?"

"If it's alright with you, ma'am, I think I would prefer to sit out here on your porch. I'll let you ladies visit."

"O.K.," Anna glanced back at him as they went inside. He had dropped into a rocker and already seemed lost in thought as he stared across the ranch.

"He's been this way since he got back," Mrs. Wilson's voice wavered as she talked.

"Is this your grandson who was in the war?"

"Yes, he just got back a few weeks ago and he's having trouble readjusting to civilian life. Post Traumatic something, they called it."

"P.T.S.D.," Anna corrected her. "That's what Nathan had this past year."

"I wasn't sure, but I thought maybe it was the same thing." Mrs. Wilson shook her head as she stared at the table. "I don't know what I can do to help him. He has horrible nightmares and wakes up screaming. I'm afraid to leave him alone. He has panic attacks where he's afraid to go outside. Just driving here, he said he keeps catching himself scanning the area, looking for the enemy."

Anna was shocked. She had heard of Vietnam Vets having flashbacks, but she had never thought about what it must be like to live for several years on such a high-alert status, always watching for an enemy. It must be nearly impossible to come home and just turn it off and go back to a normal life, she thought sadly. Anna described to Mrs. Wilson how Nathan had slowly come out of his shell.

"He doesn't have nightmares anymore and he's a happy little boy now, as you can see. It just takes time," Anna reassured her, "and a little Magic."

They visited for a bit, and then Mrs. Wilson said she had to get back to town. She needed to run a few errands before going home.

"I'll stop by and visit when I'm in town," Anna promised. "Maybe it'll help if I bring Magic?"

"I'm sure it will, dear."

Anna followed the elderly lady out and they both stopped short as they reached the front porch. Mike was still in the rocker, but now he had fifty pounds of black lab on his lap. Magic was curled up as if he belonged there, while Mike rocked and stroked the dog.

His face looked more relaxed, the lines of tension having eased from his forehead, an almost peaceful expression on his face. He completely ignored them as he continued stroking Magic and rocking. On and on he rocked, his strokes across Magic's back keeping time to the chair's rocking.

Both ladies turned and went quietly back inside the house and returned to the kitchen to talk.

Mike had sat down in the porch rocker while the women went inside. It may have seemed to them as if he was staring into space, but the truth was, he saw everything. He could see the boy playing with the dog and donkey from the corner of his eye, and as he stared across the ranch, he saw anything else that moved. His eyes were well trained to stare at nothing, while seeing everything. Untraining them was the problem. He saw the black dog leave his play and approach him cautiously, black tail wagging.

"Come on boy." Mike put his hand down, palm out and Magic sniffed it, then as

Mike scratched his neck, he climbed the rest of the way onto the porch, sitting down at his feet and staring up at his new friend adoringly. As he rubbed the dog's head, Magic pushed closer and closer into his leg and almost before he realized it the dog was in his lap and curled up, sleeping peacefully as Mike rocked and stroked his back. Mike hadn't even realized it, but his eyes hadn't scanned the area for at least fifteen minutes. He'd had eyes only for Magic as he rocked and rocked in his chair.

"I have an idea that might help Mike," Anna told Mrs. Wilson after they returned to the kitchen. "I'll stop by your house tomorrow if it's o.k."

"Sure, Anna."

They sat over coffee for a bit and chatted about other things, then Anna took the older woman on a tour of the house.

"Of course, we're still getting settled in, so excuse our boxes everywhere."

"No, your new home is beautiful Anna. If anyone deserved to win all that money, I'm sure it was you."

"Thank you, Mrs. Wilson. I hope Mike can bring you out often to visit."

Anna didn't follow Mrs. Wilson back outside. She could hear her talking softly to her grandson, then the car driving away.

Anna went to her new computer and began researching soldiers with P.T.S.D. She was shocked at the thousands of soldiers returning home from Iraq and Afghanistan with similar problems. And just like that, her plan for Magic Ranch was born.

Anna dropped Nathan at school the following morning, and then stopped by the animal shelter. She wasn't sure what she was looking for, until she came to a kennel with a small, multi-colored beagle staring up at her with huge brown eyes. She had a black and white body with a mostly brown head and long, brown ears.

"Her name is Molly," the worker explained. "She was a family pet, but when the family moved to Denver, I guess they had no room for a dog." Anna could hear a note of anger in the lady's tone.

"Is she well-behaved?" Anna asked.

"She seems to be. She's quiet and a little shy."

"Perfect." Anna smiled. "I'll take her."

When Anna reached Mrs. Wilson's trailer, she picked Molly up and carried her inside.

Mike was sitting on the couch, staring at the

T.V. until she placed the small dog in his lap.

He looked startled at first, and then began softly stroking Molly's head as he saw the fear in the dog's eyes.

"Her name is Molly," Anna told him. "If you can bring her by the ranch in the afternoons, I'm sure Nathan would be happy to help you train her. She's sad and lonely and needs a lot of love right now. Can I count on you, Mike?"

"Yes, ma'am," Mike's voice was soft as he answered, he looked up at her with a look of joy and wonder on his face.

Mrs. Wilson followed Anna back to her car.

"I can't thank you enough, Anna. I can't bear seeing my only grandson suffering this way."

"You're very welcome," Anna hugged her, "I just hope it helps."

Chapter 20

Over the next month, Mike began coming by the ranch every day.

He began helping Brian with chores around the ranch, Molly always at his heels. Everyone helped with Molly's training, including Lisa, who had found a friend in Mike. They seemed awkward and untrusting around each other at first, but they formed a friendship based on their kindred spirit. Lisa sensed Mike's pain and suffering, she followed him around the ranch, much as Molly did. Mike was annoyed and distrusting of her at first, but her tenacious attitude won him over in the end.

Lisa was helping him rebuild the corral fence one chilly day, when Mike suddenly stopped and asked her if she'd like to take a break and go for a walk.

"I'd love to," she told him with a big smile.

He'd acted so gruff with her over the past month, she was thrilled that he was beginning to loosen up.

Nathan was at school and Magic was lying dejectedly on the porch, waiting for him. When he saw Mike and Lisa start off across the field, Molly at their heels, he left the porch and joined them. Lisa almost had to jog to match Mike's long, businesslike stride.

"Hey, slow down," she caught up to him and grabbed his arm. "We're not on a forced march here, just relax."

He looked down at her and chuckled, then slowed his pace to match hers. Lisa kept her arm tucked in his as they strolled. She found it strange, she knew this man was a trained killing machine, yet she wasn't afraid of him. She sensed a gentleness under his hard, disciplined military exterior.

They walked down to the creek and took a seat in the grass as the dogs played and sniffed along the bank. They sat quietly for a bit, listening to the sound the water made as it ran across the stones.

Lisa was surprised when Mike started talking. He'd been so quiet around her, almost surly.

"I had a friend in boot camp named Jeff," he began slowly, keeping his eyes on the moving water.

"We got to know each other pretty well, then kinda lost touch after basic. Then, when I got to my base in Afghanistan, there he was. We were in the same unit. We picked up our friendship right where we left off. You become like brothers, over there. We depend on each other for our very lives."

Lisa nodded when he paused.

"I actually slept better over there than I have since coming home," he went on.

"There's always someone on guard duty…watching our backs, you know. Now I get back here and there's no one. The first few weeks back, I mostly laid there, staring at the ceiling, listening to the night sounds."

"Yeah," Lisa said softly. "I know the feeling."

"I thought so," Mike nodded, and then

went on. "Well, Jeff told me when I arrived that he'd met this girl in town and he'd been sneaking off to see her. He said he was madly in love with her and he wanted to help her get to the States. I had only been there a week when Jeff woke me up, saying he was slipping off to town. Our unit was out on patrol and we were sleeping in the desert. Well, I heard him, but I wasn't really awake, you know what I mean?" Lisa nodded.

"I think I mumbled something, then rolled over. It was late and I was exhausted. The next thing I knew, we heard something like a bomb go off, then rifle fire. We all jumped up and we could see Jeff on his back, a few hundred yards away, and our night guard was down, but he was alive and returning rifle fire toward a sandy hill. We fired toward it too, and we called for a helicopter, but it didn't arrive til daylight."

"Jeff was just lying there," Mike's voice broke and he paused, then cleared his throat before continuing.

"He called out to me for help but every time I would try to move toward him, bullets would hit all around me. We were really just pinned down at our camp until help arrived."

He cleared his throat again, then went on, "I tried to save him…I swear I did. But all I could do was sit there helpless, listening to him call my name. It was only a couple hours til the sun came up and the chopper arrived, but it was too late for Jeff."

Lisa saw a single tear roll slowly down Mike's face.

"I just let him die," he said, his voice breaking with the pain. "I should have died trying to save him."

Lisa pulled him into her arms without speaking and held him. "It's not your fault." She rubbed his back and held onto him as he tried to pull away. "It's not your fault," she repeated. She said it again and again until he repeated it.

Finally, he pulled away and turned his eyes back to the water, but he kept her small hand in his.

"I still have nightmares and wake up screaming," he said quietly. "But it's getting better. Molly seems to sense when I'm having a nightmare and she jumps on my chest and licks my face until I wake up. I think Anna saved my life with that little dog. I owe her a debt of gratitude that I'll never be able to repay."

"Me too," Lisa told Mike her own story and about Anna's visits to the hospital.

"Even though Magic belongs to Nathan, he's been my savior," she said.

"I think Magic belongs to everyone," Mike chuckled. "I never knew that pets could have such a healing magic about them."

"Me either," Lisa smiled, her small hand still captured in his.

Anna watched the friendship between Mike and Lisa grow day by day, often wondering if she was watching the first stages of romance. They reminded her of herself and Brian, such a short time ago.

Meanwhile, she hired a contractor to turn some of the empty horse stalls into dog pens, with a fenced run outside so the dogs could go in and out. She had been contacting Veteran's hospitals in Colorado and neighboring states, getting the word out about Magic Ranch.

She paid Mike and Lisa to paint the huge red barn, then checked around at different shelters until she found just the right dogs. She brought three home with her over the weeks, a German Shepherd, a Golden Retriever and a black and a white Border Collie. She needed something to call them by; she named the retriever Liberty, the shepherd Justice, and the border collie, the only female and Anna's personal favorite, she called MIA, in honor of all American soldiers missing in action. She hoped the soldiers who eventually took the dogs home would give them names they chose themselves, but for now they used the names she'd given them to begin their obedience training. Everyone pitched in with their training; they needed quiet, easy-going, well-behaved dogs for healing ex-soldiers. Mia was well-behaved, but so energetic that Anna could see she would need more training than the others. Anna was hopeful that her plan would work and she could be saving two lives at once.

"You're doing a good thing here," Mike told her one day as they stood at the railing of the training yard, watching Lisa and Nathan with Mia. "If you help even one returning soldier the way Molly's helped me, it'll make all the effort worthwhile."

"I think we can, Mike, and I have more ideas for things we can do. I would like to have a facility here for kids, too." She described the therapy ranch they'd been to in Colorado Springs.

"Sounds great, Anna. I would be happy to help any way I can."

"You want to make it a full time job?"

"Are you serious?" His face lit up with pleasure. "I would love it."

Lisa was feeding the dogs in their new pens in the barn on a cold, windy day in January when she heard footsteps behind her. She assumed it was Mike until she stood up, patted the dog's head and turned, straight into the arms of her husband, Joe. He was a big, burly man with beefy arms covered in dark hair.

He grabbed her upper arms and began shaking her. She could smell alcohol on his breath. It even seemed to seep from his pores, he had a sour, sickening smell about him.

"You got me arrested, then ran away," he screamed in her face as he shook her. "I told you what would happen if you left me, didn't I?" He pushed her away from him, and then backhanded her across the face. The force of the blow knocked her to the floor of the barn. She pulled herself up to a sitting position and rubbed her hand across her mouth where he'd hit her. Her hand came away bloody. She had been half-expecting this for months. He'd always promised her that he'd find her if she left him.

The dogs in the pens were barking furiously as he advanced on her, his hands drawn into fists. He dropped onto her, straddling her waist as he punched her again and again. Lisa screamed and brought her hands up, trying to protect her face. Joe suddenly let out a yelp of shock and surprise as Magic ran into the barn, jumped and slammed into his back, knocking him off Lisa. Magic backed away slowly, showing his teeth, a low growl coming from deep in his chest. Joe scrambled to his feet and, as he rose, Mike's fist slammed into his face.

Mike had been heading to the barn, looking for Lisa, when he heard her scream. Joe had gone down with Mike's first punch and Mike leaped onto the bigger man and pummeled his face with his fists. A white hot rage overtook him when he realized this was the man who had almost killed Lisa before. He put his knee on Joe's chest and grabbed his throat. The big man brought both beefy hands up, grabbing Mike's hand and trying to pull it away. Mike only increased his pressure until he felt a hand on his shoulder. He looked up and Brian was standing over him.

"That's enough, Mike." Brian said quietly, keeping his hand on Mike's shoulder.

Mike felt his rage slipping away as he returned to his senses. He released his grip on Joe's neck and slowly stood up, looking at Lisa.

She was still sitting on the floor and she was still looking at Joe, terror etching lines across her face.

Mike followed her gaze and saw Joe with a pistol pointed at Lisa and his finger was squeezing the trigger. Mike's military training kicked in and he kicked the pistol from Joe's hand. The pistol clattered to the floor between them and Mike leaped, grabbing for the pistol before Joe could pick it up. Mike came up with the pistol, but Joe had pulled a knife from a boot holster. Brian heard the pistol fire at the same time he heard a grunt from Mike.

Joe fell over and remained still, a red stain spreading across his plaid shirt. Mike was pulling the three-inch blade from his abdomen as Brian rushed to him, dropping down and holding his hand over the wound, blood running through his fingers.

"Call 911," he yelled at Lisa. It brought her out of her immobilized terror. She turned and ran for the house, screaming for Anna.

Brian, Anna and Lisa were sitting in Mike's hospital room when he woke up. He'd had surgery to repair the wound in his stomach from Joe's knife. He was in the capable hands of Nurse Davies and Anna had no doubt he'd recover completely.

Lisa took his big hand in hers as he opened his eyes. Mike smiled at her as she leaned over him, his smile turning to a frown as he saw the purple bruises on Lisa's face.

"Is he dead?" His voice was a dry croak,

but Lisa heard. She nodded her head as her tears spilled over.

"You saved my life, Mike. Thank you." She leaned over and kissed his lips gently.

"We have a surprise for you," Anna said. She leaned down and picked up Molly, who'd been sleeping at her feet and placed her gently on the bed beside Mike.

"Down," Anna put her hand palm out to Molly as she spoke and the dog lay down happily beside Mike, licking his hand. Mike stroked her head and with his free hand, took Lisa's hand and pulled her down on the bed too.

Brian wrapped an arm around Anna's shoulder and they quietly backed out of the room.

Mike recovered quickly under the excellent care of Nurse Davies.

Lisa didn't want to leave him the first couple days. Nurse Davies had a cot brought into his room and Lisa stayed by his side around the clock.

Anna visited every day, bringing Molly with her. She also brought Magic a couple times and visited other patients at the hospital.

Mike was back at the ranch after a few days and staying in Lisa's cottage. She wanted to take care of him while he healed and she wouldn't take no for an answer. She owed him a huge debt for saving her life and it was the least she could do.

Anna was outside working with the dogs one chilly day with Lisa, Mike and Nathan when Brian came strolling up to her. He grabbed her into a bear hug as he reached her and swung her in a circle as everyone laughed. Magic ran around their ankles barking and Nathan ran over for a hug, too.

"Swing me, too," he squealed in delight as Brian swung him around the yard, then they all stood together, his arms around them both, watching Lisa and Mike working amiably together with the dogs.

"Now this, babe, this is the real American dream," Brian said as he held them both to him, swinging his free arm wide to encompass their new friends, their old farmhouse and the stunning vista before them.

This book was written while traveling across
America, listening to news stories of families
struggling during the recession, people losing
everything to natural disasters and servicemen
arriving home with P.T.S.D. Through the
struggles of my own family and the stories of
others, I learned that the real 'American Dream,'
is not about a house or what kind of car
you drive, but about family and love and
enjoying life.